I DO (NO'T)

AT THE RODEO

ALICE VL

I DO (NOT) – AT THE RODEO

Alice VL

Copyright 2018

I DO (NOT)

Part 3

AT THE RODEO

Alice VL

I DO (NOT) – AT THE RODEO

HOWDY!

Howdy! It's me, Ally Bradshaw. *sigh*

In true Southern style, my story picks up when I head back to my childhood home in Water Hills, Constantia to spend a supposed rehabilitating, re-orienting, re-educating and what I suspect a kind of exorcism three weeks with my parents. *sigh* I am so excited … whoop freaking whoop. Just kidding! This is basically the worst thing in my life at the moment and could not have come at a worse time.

To say the least, my dad, Jason is a rather tense and edgy man in his early sixties. Ever since my brother Max passed away at the age of nineteen, my father has been nothing short of over-protective and controlling. He serves as a Deacon in our Church in the town I grew up in and can be just a tad bit overpowering. My mom, Sylvia staunchly supports him and would never contradict my dad's will or authority. Not that she doesn't have one of her own. She loves him and the life they have in Water Hills. She just loves that she is a perfect Southern lady and that her family is just peachy. That leaves me, Ally. The good girl turned bad. Bad'ish. In their eyes, and thanks to Michael. Jerk.

But, on a more positive note, what perfect timing to go home to my parents? Water Hills kicks off with their week-long

I DO (NOT) – AT THE RODEO

Annual Fall Festival on the very day I get there. That means eight-second men, rodeo events, cowboys, fairs, rides *oh boy* and late-night country music festivities. Yay! But, it also means Church and it means dealing with my parents and the aftermath of my not-so-proper encounter with Michael.

I haven't heard a single word from him or Lily since that fateful morning. He hasn't shown up at the museum or at my apartment, so I am holding my breath and hoping that my plan wasn't so flawed after all. Except for the fact that I must now sit through three weeks of torture with my parents, I think I did pretty good. Michael knows my parents and he knows the trouble I'm in with them. Blah. Blah.

As I sit here writing this, I must be honest, I am still fixated on Daniel. I like the idea of having him around; I just don't like the fact that he could quite possibly be dating by the time I get back. I know. I'm such a hypocrite. But still. I like Daniel, I enjoy his company and so does the rest of me. What can I say?

My encounters with William were amazing. Different. My ventures and excursions with him were wonderfully eye-opening and I am more in touch with what tickles me, what I like, and what I don't like which is pretty much nothing. More than ever before, I am realizing that I am actually still, a plain country girl who does not want romance, and I still come from dirt roads and boots. Not that there was anything I disliked about William, but Daniel is more my thing. If you can call it that? Okay, I am probably more in tune with my body's little sensor switches if you must.

Bianca will be keeping an eye on my place while I'm in

the country. I am going to do my best to get through the coming three weeks when it comes to behaving myself, or at least, appear to be the same good daughter I was, and convince my parents that I am still Ally. Their little girl. Their pride and joy. Their obedient, loving, caring and classy little good girl, who just starting saying fuck a lot. I'm not holding my breath though. My mother can see right through me. She always does.

'Yeah right, Ally. All you have on your mind are the eight-second rodeo riders and those damn sizzling cowboys!'

So, here I am driving into Water Hills. This is where my three-week adventure, or catastrophe kicks off, and this is how it plays out.

Call me whatever you like, just don't call me drab, boring or ugly.

Ally.

Alice VL

I DO (NOT) – AT THE RODEO

PART 1

Driving into Water Hills was bittersweet for me. I used to walk these streets with my brother Max when we were children. First when we were elementary schoolers, and then as teenagers. Despite the fact that we were slightly caged in by our parents, we had a wonderful childhood right here in the country, and even though we clashed tremendously with our parents, I can hardly imagine having grown up anywhere else.

Besides the fact that our parents were strict disciplinarians who took pride in our family and the fact that we were well-raised, well-adjusted and obedient children, we did have a happy, well-balanced, loving and normal childhood.

Max was the carefree, funny, slightly reckless and hauntingly attractive of the two of us. He turned into a bit of a rebel when he reached his teens, but nonetheless, he was the guy with the biggest of hearts. My mother hovered around him, the apple of her eye, while I was more daddy's girl. There was very little Max could do wrong in both my parents' eyes, and he often took advantage of his 'favorite-child' status.

But, he turned out to be a good man and was still so young when he was killed in a car crash. My parents were grief-stricken, devastated and wholly debilitated after losing their only son. My mom refused to get out of bed on most days after the accident, and my dad spent more time in Church than on the farm. That left me without not only my brother, but my parents. Alone. With each day that passed after Max's death, I spent more time on my own feeling as though I was invisible to not only my parents, but to the entire world.

I remember standing in the doorway of my parents' bedroom and hearing my mom cry for Max. She would cry for hours and hours in the darkness and even though it was crushing to witness, I understood how she felt. She was Max's mother, and I, only his sister. It hurt like hell. The loss and grief I felt after Max had died came in grueling, appetite-losing, sleep-depriving waves. Some days, it would dull a little but other days, it felt as though death was coming for me too. We as a family, were never the same again.

What was once whole, was shattered and destroyed. Peace turned to emptiness and sadness turned to rage. My parents would argue with one another over the littlest of things, leaving me to hide out in my bedroom until the storm had calmed. I would grab Max's guitar and begin slamming on the strings until my palms hurt and my fingers bled. I didn't want to hear them argue and blame one another, but more than anything, I was so afraid Max would hear them too.

I hated it.

I hated that Max died and left me alone with them. I hated that my mother never smiled again, but more than that, I hated that my father sat out on the porch until long after my mother fell asleep at night, not wanting to face her and not wanting to listen to her cry in her sleep.

I couldn't stand seeing the agony they both were in and I often wished that I was in the car instead of Max. I would probably had done anything to change places with him and often, I still feel that way. I still think Max would have figured this whole life thing out better than I have. I, on my own, just was never enough to keep my parents going. I was never enough to live for.

It was as though Max was the one to bring oxygen into their souls, and love into our home. Even though he would clear out the fridge by his inexplicable appetite after spending hours at the gym, I could never fault him and saw him as my mentor even that he was always poking fun at me. But, he was my big brother; the one who would disengage and disarm my bullies effortlessly. He would walk me to class each day as a way to show the mean girls that he had my back. Yes, he was my worst enemy at times, but when it all came down to it, Max was my very best friend. Max was fiercely loyal and protective of all that he loved. Actually, all that were vulnerable.

When I met Michael, I sort of felt as though I belonged again. Somewhere. To someone. I felt that I meant something, even if only to one person. I was swept off my feet and began looking forward to leaving the farmhouse, my parents behind and all the anguish behind me. I was happy again. I missed Max. I missed the freedom I lost when Max died but what I didn't realize at the time was that I was simply swapping one prison for another.

So naturally, when Michael and I began dating, I was only permitted to be out and about if I was accompanied by him. My

Alice VL

parents grew fond of Michael very early on and shortly after we began dating. I often thought that they were trying to replace the hole left behind by Max, by filling it with Michael. Their replacement son. My mother never missed an opportunity to remind me of how lucky I was that Michael had chosen me.

And I did feel lucky. I couldn't believe that he had chosen me and often, I'd pinch myself to make sure I wasn't dreaming. I fell in love with Michael early on, but in retrospect, I am pretty sure I fell in love with the promise of freedom and a life away from my parents and their misery.

I know. It all sounds terrible. Don't get me wrong; they're not bad people and are loving, generous and kind parents, but their sorrow just short of destroyed what was left of our family. We were all living from day to day in a misty fog; a wandering haze. Every single day. I felt stuck, every single day.

I couldn't speak to my mother anymore, and when I sat out on the porch with my father, he stubbornly sat staring out onto the fields in front of him without saying a word and without as much as a 'how are you doing, Ally?' Nothing. They both had an unhealthy, distant look in their eyes and would only communicate with the world and each other if it was absolutely necessary. I hated it. For a long time afterwards, I hated Max for being so stupid by getting himself killed.

When I left to move to Willow County with Michael, my dad was once again, heartbroken. He despised the fact that I was moving so far away from home, but in the same breath, he was satisfied that I was in supposed good hands. Yeah, whatever.

Michael was never a terrible husband. Throughout our

entire marriage, he was civilized and decent. But, Michael was cold, distant and self-absorbed. He was extremely critical of my appearance, my attitude and my vocabulary. I hated that too, but I put up with it because I loved him. Or did I? Perhaps, I just thought I did. Actually, that's exactly what it was.

Enough of this useless information. I was almost home. I slowed down slightly when I recognized the tree-lined driveway that leads directly to our farmhouse. As I drove through the driveway, I felt a sudden quiver in my heart. It is a beautiful place. The homestead was built on a slight rise that gradually sloped away on each side. There were rows and rows of trees that lined the trail leading up to our home and at the back, my mother's vegetable garden was her pride and joy as well as the dozen horses she adores and cares for as though they were her children.

There are acres and acres of farm land where my dad keeps cattle, sheep and chickens to keep his days full and his mind off of Max.

My mother loves lavender and I could already smell the scents that would greet me as I walked into our home. She never aspired to a large house, preferring a cozy and warm home. There was no shortage of space for the four of us, and my mom would often refer to it as her bungalow in the sky. She furnished our house with everything old and rustic and had a magnificent eye for art. It was truly nothing more than a simple space, until my mother brought her personality into it, made her mark and made our home.

She teaches children to ride, specifically children or adults that have been through some sort of trauma in their lives.

I DO (NOT) – AT THE RODEO

My mother is a staunch supporter and firm believer that horses provide therapy to any tortured or demon-infested soul. I know. Demon-infested? But she wholeheartedly believes in the therapy, and it had most certainly helped her fill some of the void Max's death left her with.

My horse named Tinkerbell, died about four years ago, but not before she left me with a filly, Bleu. Max's horse, Martial passed away a little over a year after his accident which left my mom and dad crushed and mourning him all over again. The universe was unkind to my parents as it snatched from them what they weren't willing to let go of, one by one. Max was far too young, and Martial was far too special, but death didn't care. It hung over my parents for much too long and left them feeling as though everything and everyone they loved were threatened. Death had ripped away a part of her almost as though it was extinguishing Max's very existence.

When I finally pulled up in front of the farmhouse, I noticed my dad on the porch, sipping his beer and smoking a cigar. Nothing had changed. Nothing was different. It was like stepping back into ten years ago and all I could do was shake my head and let out an enormous sigh.

'How some things just haunt you forever.'

It was as though time had stood still in Water Hills. The hours passed, the days went by, but time, it all just stood still. Nobody moved forward. Nobody changed or moved on with the times. Nobody wanted to. Life in Water Hills reminded me of a movie from the early 1940's. The buildings had never been updated, except for a fresh coat of paint each year, and the town's traditions have remained unchanged throughout the years.

My father waved when he spotted me park my car and immediately got up to greet me. I was happy to see him, and when I looked into his eyes, I knew without a doubt that I missed my dad.

"Hello Princess."

"Hello daddy …"

I flung my arms tightly around him and rested my head on his chest. I had forgotten what a giant of a man my dad is. He is tall, sturdy and strong, and it made me happy to see that he had hardly aged a single day since I saw him last, but he looked tired.

"Did you have any problems on the road?"

"No problems dad. I left early, so I missed most of the morning traffic."

"It's good to have you home."

"It's good to be home, daddy. I've missed you."

"I've missed you too, princess."

I just have to say, when my dad calls me princess, I melt. Despite his ways, and despite his unreasonable demands at times, I love him. I feel safe and shielded when my father's arms are around me. I am glad I came, even if the moment is fleeting.

"Your mother is inside."

I DO (NOT) – AT THE RODEO

Sigh My dad frowned and glared at me all at the same time.

"Oh Ally, she misses you."

"Yeah right."

"Ally Bradshaw!"

"Sorry dad."

"Let me help you get your bags so you can go inside and greet your mother."

Hand in hand, we walked over to the trunk of my car. My dad took out the oversized and overstuffed suitcase, while I pulled out a smaller sling bag.

With my handbag clutched in one hand, my sling bag in the other, I marched bravely behind my father up the steps of the porch and into the farmhouse. I didn't really know what to expect from my mother. I never do.

Our relationship has been rocky for years. We have been clashing for as long as I can remember and to be honest, it began long before Max died but was never as intense as it was then. After Max's death, I often wondered if given the chance, would she trade me for Max? But, what I couldn't deny was the fact that she loved me, even though she no longer knew how to love me.

And, I love her even if I don't agree with her most of the time. We would clash endlessly, but I love her. She is my mother.

When we walked in, I could smell the whiffs of my

mother's freshly baked cakes and pies coming from the kitchen. Any person stepping into my mother's kitchen for the first time, could confuse it for a bakery. So much of the house was converted to create the space my mother needed to bake mouth-watering cakes, pies and biscuits and now that the festival was here, it was all she did.

'Aah yes, the Annual Fall Festival begins tonight.'

I was excited to spend my first evening in Constantia at the festival. It was a tradition that had been going on for over a hundred years and it normally lasts a total of seven days. That meant that for seven days and six nights, we were permanent fixtures at the festival. For as long as I could remember, my mother sold pies and cakes at a little stall that was surrounded by other kiosks selling arts, crafts, and just about anything you can think of. As she had been doing every other year before, she would donate the proceeds of her sales to the poor and the needy. My dad on the other hand, would round up our horses and ponies to the fair, and take children out on horseback rides.

When my father was younger, he diligently participated in all the yearly rodeo tournaments that came to Water Hills. As a little girl, I would climb onto the rails and watch my father on bulls and horses as he kicked off the nightly events. True to his nature, he would stare from under his wide-brimmed hat as his eyes narrowed and his one hand gripped onto the saddle while tossing his other hand into the air. For eight seconds, my dad would be battered and bruised by the mightiest of bulls, but never once was he thrown off.

When he retired a few years ago, he retired as the

reigning eight-second champion of the state and inducted into the cowboy division of the hall of fame. My father is known in Constantia as one of the last true cowboys and many articles have been written and printed on his legacy; one the world had hoped Max would step into.

I, on the other hand, spent my teenage years at the festival gawking and drooling over the eight-second cowboys. Yes, I know. I never really noticed that I used to do drivel so shamelessly, until now. I am rather ashamed to admit that my appreciation of an etched, shaped and good-looking man started long before I even met Daniel. 'Oh Lord. Enough.' Back to my mother. Back to being proper and back to being daddy's little princess.

I stepped carefully and slowly into the kitchen, and smiled nervously when my mother turned around to face me. She was wearing an apron over a summer dress, her hair was tied back, but I couldn't help but notice the worn-out and exhausted expression in her eyes. It looked as though my mother had aged a hundred years since the last time I saw her. I mean, knew she was still struggling to come to terms with Max's death, but what I didn't count on was how visible her grief would still be. My heart hurt for her. At that very moment, I would have done anything to bring Max back to her. I was prepared to plead, beg and negotiate anything with God and the universe, to bring Max back to her.

"Ally Bradshaw, it's about time you came home for a visit … why must we always resort to threats?"

"Happy to be home, mama."

I lied. Sort of. She made me nervous, but despite the

discomfort between us, I was truly happy to see them both again. My dad took the sling bag that was still dangling over my shoulder, clutched my suitcase, and smiled warmly,

"I am going to put these upstairs in your old room."

"Thank you, daddy."

When he disappeared down the passage, I turned back to my mother who was pouring us each a cup of tea. I hesitantly took a seat at the kitchen table, and quickly pulled out my mobile phone from my handbag. I promised Bianca that I'd let her know when I got there, and I didn't want her to worry.

I noticed a flickering light on my mobile phone, and immediately assumed it was Bianca checking up on me, already panicky about whether I had arrived safely. To my shock, I realized that it was not Bianca, but Daniel. My heart immediately broke out into a flutter and frenziedly began galloping as each thump left me short of breath. I did not expect a message from him.

'Are you safe?'

I tried my best not to smile, but there was no way in the world I could disguise my utter delight at Daniel's message.

'Just got here. Thanks for asking.'

I quickly scrolled down to Bianca's name and sent her a text,

'Here. Miss you already.'

Alice VL

I DO (NOT) – AT THE RODEO

I hit send and before I placed my phone on the kitchen table, a new message came through from Daniel.

'Wish you were here.'

'Me too.'

The phone bleeped once again. This time, it was Bianca.

'Enjoy. And have mercy on those poor suckers over there.'

I giggled before I finally placed the phone down in front of me.

"I hope you won't be on that thing the entire time you're here?"

My mother's condescending tone just knew exactly how to hurl me into a sudden, unavoidable unpleasant and murky mood,

"I was just letting my friends know I got here safely."

"Yes well. We need to talk about that too."

"What? About my friends? Mother, I have been here for five minutes and you are already having me wish I didn't come. I am thirty-one years old. You do know that, right?"

She placed our tea on the table, followed by a tray of sandwiches. Tiny little triangle cut sandwiches, and I could have bet you a million bucks before I saw them that they were cucumber and mayo sandwiches. Yep, spot on.

Alice VL

I DO (NOT) – AT THE RODEO

"I don't care how old you are, Ally. You are my daughter. You are still a Channing and I won't have you blemish our good name or tarnish your good reputation."

'Ha! My good reputation!' I wanted to blurt it out and tell her all about Daniel and William, just for the hell of it, but I was at once relieved that my dad walked in and sat down at the head of the table.

"Mama ..."

He whispered softly before he placed a hand over my mother's hand as she slowly sat down.

"Not now ... let the girl at least have her tea and sandwiches first."

'Thank the Lord. Hallelujah!'

My mother handed us each a cup of tea, and in an awkward, unnerving silence, we ate our sandwiches. When I began sipping my tea, she could no longer contain her irritation or keep a single word left for later or even better, unsaid. She placed her cup of tea down in front of her, and turned to face me squarely in the eye,

"What's all this about Michael?"

My dad leaned back after he placed a half-eaten sandwich back on his plate and pushed it away. He folded his hands out in front of him and appeared to be aggravated at once. I was not sure if it was exasperation for me, or for my mother. I couldn't really tell if I could decipher the tensed expression on his face.

I DO (NOT) – AT THE RODEO

"Michael lied, mom. I did not drug him. I would never drug him. I don't even know where to find the drugs to drug him with. I wish I did though …"

'Oops.'

"Then why would he lie to us about it? Why on earth would he come up with such a story, Ally? We've known Michael for a long time."

"And you, mama … you've known me my entire life … can you honestly say that you believe I would do that?"

I was sad. Hurt. Angry. Disappointed. I was reeling and enraged all at the same time.

"Give me one good reason why Michael would lie?"

"I don't know why he would go that far, mom? Maybe to cover up his own tracks, or maybe to get me into trouble with you and dad? He cheated on me. With my best friend and in our bed … you don't seem as agitated by that?"

I sighed and placed my cup of tea on the table. I doubted whether I would ever get through to my mother.

"He just doesn't leave me alone. He phones. He texts. He comes by my work and apartment unannounced and more often than not, after I am in bed or before I wake up. He complains about Lily, about life and about everything else. He just shows up. All I want is a chance to start my life over again. I don't want Michael in my life anymore. And the reason I did what I did and take note, I did not drug him, was because I was sick and tired of it. It should worry you more that it was so easy to get him in such a compromising position …"

"Alright Ally. Say you didn't drug him, how did the whole naked thing come about?"

"Sylva … do we have to do this now? Ally hasn't driven for hours just to walk into an ambush!"

'Wait. Hang on. My dad is sticking up for me? Why?'

"You know what, dad? Let's do this now. Let's get this all out of the way now because if I am expected to spend the next three weeks like this, I'll rather go home. And no, you and mom are not welcome to follow me home. Alright?"

My mother glared at me. My heart was racing. My blood was pumping and boiling all at the same time. 'Fuck you, Michael.'

"He came by just after five that morning. A Saturday morning. Without Lily. For supposed coffee. That was his excuse, coffee. He wouldn't take no for an answer, so, I blindfolded him and tied him up. He was willing, ready and believe me, dad, so able. He thought we were going to have sex. Do you really think I am strong enough to blindfold and tie Michael up on my own, even if I drugged him?"

"Say I believe you. Why would you stoop so low, Ally?"

My mother had an instant look of disgust on her face for me. That was exactly the look I had grown accustomed to whenever she looked at me. It hurt and infuriated me all at once.

"Because mom … I wanted him to stop coming by. You're

not listening to me; I found him in my bed with Lily, and God alone knows how long it went on for? I just wanted to teach him a lesson."

My dad placed a hand over mine, and leaned slightly forward,

"Don't bring God into this, Ally. He has nothing to do with this.

"Sorry dad. I didn't mean it like that."

"Well Ally, I don't approve of the way you handled yourself or the situation with Michael. His family and ours have been friends for many years and this has left both sides embarrassed. There are other ways to deal with things like that. That was so unlike you?"

"No, it wasn't unlike me, Mom. This is exactly who I am."

My mother's irritation was progressing. I could see it on her face and when the corners of her mouth curved downwards, I knew without a doubt that she was ashamed of me.

"Michael says you were out with another man?"

I almost choked on my tea. 'Seriously?'

"Yes, I was out with another man and to be honest, I've been out with two men since the divorce, and now that I'm here … hopefully, it will be three. And if I'm really lucky … it could be four or perhaps, more."

"Ally Bradshaw!"

I DO (NOT) – AT THE RODEO

I know. That was uncalled for. Inappropriate and rude. That was unlike me, and I regretted saying that almost at once. It was just that my mother knew exactly which buttons to push. Never before had I spoken to her like that, and it was shocking, even to me.

"Sorry dad."

I cared what my father thought. I cared about his opinion of me and how I reflected in his eyes. I didn't want him to think of me like that, but at the same time, Sylvia Channing was working on my last nerve.

As though she could tell what I was thinking, she tensely excused herself and immediately got up from the kitchen table. Without saying another word, she began clearing away the dishes. My father was agitated, and when he got up, he shook his head and walked out to I assumed, the porch. He was always on the porch.

"Go unpack your things. The Annual Fall Festival begins tonight. I expect you will accompany us?"

My mother snapped at me but did not look in my direction again.

"Wouldn't miss it for the world."

I meant it. It was the one thing I was sincerely happy about. I couldn't wait to get away from her and when I walked out of the kitchen, I was instantly relieved that the 'Michael' discussion had been dealt with. Sort of. At least, I hoped it had been dealt with for once and for all.

Alice VL

I DO (NOT) – AT THE RODEO

Before unpacking my suitcase, I wanted to check on my father and when I reached the porch, I sat down on an empty chair next to him, "Sorry about back there, dad."

"You don't have to apologize, my girl. Can I tell you a secret?"

Wait. Hang on. I don't have to apologize? Since when? My heart came alive and I was instantly intrigued,

"Yes?"

"If you ever tell your mother, I'll deny it, but I never liked Michael. I always thought you could do better. I have always felt that he was beneath you. Don't get me wrong, I have much respect for his family, but Michael … nah uh."

"Are you for real, dad? I mean, really?"

He took my hand into his and gently squeezed it,

"I do. And if you want to date a million frogs before you find your prince, then so be it. As long as you're happy, my girl. I don't care what the town thinks, and I certainly don't care about keeping up appearances. I am too old for this shit."

'Wait. Hang on. My dad is on my side? Why?'

"Wow dad. I did not see that coming. What's going on with you?"

"I suppose I'm just getting old, my girl. I suppose we handled things wrong after Max died. We weren't there for you like we should have been and I think what your mother and I failed to see, was your grief. You were grieving just as we were and for that, I am sorry. I love you my princess, and I don't care about much of anything except your happiness"

I was shocked and could feel the tears sting in my eyes. I was stunned. Thrown. Completely caught off-guard.

"I don't know what to say … love you, daddy."

There was nothing else I could think of saying to him at that very moment. There was so much inside of me that had been wanting to come out for so long, but when I leaned my head against his shoulder, I quickly wiped the tears from my eyes and decided to remain quiet.

"Just be patient with your mother. And please my Ally girl, no scandals while you're here, okay? Or rather, don't get caught out in any …"

I giggled softly still resting my head against his shoulder. I couldn't help but wonder if my father perhaps secretly knew what I had been up to. Did he know how that his daughter, Ally Bradshaw had become obsessed with her own sensuality and embarked on one slutty encounter after another? I hope not.

Could he know about Daniel or William?

Alice VL

I DO (NOT) – AT THE RODEO

PART 2

When it was time to leave for the Annual Fall Festival, I slid into the front seat of my father's truck and took my place in between my parents. Just as I used to when I was a little girl. I was dressed in a strappy summer's dress, but I threw on a sweater just in case. It was a chilly, windy afternoon and most certainly, an indication that fall was well underway.

I was eagerly looking forward to the festivities but more than that, I couldn't wait to hang out at the rodeo and attend the first barn dance of the season later that night.

That was the one thing I could do, and do well. For a long time, it was the only way my body truly knew how to speak while my mouth remained verbally guarded. Usually, the soft toys that were neatly stacked on my bed were my only audience, but later and as I grew older, I would dance in the barns amongst my mother's horses.

It was my escape from my parents' silence and was almost as though I was able to turn back the clock; back to a time when we were happy. My life as a daughter of grieving parents was all about obligation, duty and deference that never could sit well with my soul. Dancing, music, horses and soft toys were my only escape and one I welcomed with open arms.

Alice VL

I DO (NOT) – AT THE RODEO

When we pulled up at the festival, my dad quickly climbed out and unpacked the truck. My mother and I helped him carry in all the goodies my mom had baked. Carrying a pie and a cake in each hand, I followed them out to their stall.

I was excited to see our horses again. I couldn't wait to lose myself in the crowds of thousands of people, away from my mother who had barely said a word to me since our little confrontation around the kitchen table earlier on.

Once the tables had been set up, the cakes and pies were displayed, my father unexpectedly took my hand,

"Let's go see the horses."

"I'd love to, dad."

I squeezed his hand gently before we strolled over to the open fields, a short distance from where my mother had begun selling her cakes and pies. When we reached the riding field, I was happy to see children taking turns on the horses. They were faces of pure and utter joy; little humans that were having a blast as they went around and around the make-shift riding track my dad had built.

"Mr. Channing!"

My dad and I both turned around at once when I noticed a man running up to meet us. It seemed urgent, and he sounded breathless. I squinted my eyes and tried to look past the glare of the sun and when he finally came closer, I was instantly unprepared for a smile that was beginning to form around my mouth. Unintentionally. Unconsciously. Call it whatever you want, but I just had the biggest smile on my face. Even from a distance, I could tell that he was most certainly not your average cowboy.

His dark, shoulder length hair was blowing in the wind as he came running up to us. His jeans were ripped, and his blue checked shirt hung slightly over his waistline. A waist coat, a brown cowboy hat and boots indicating a pair of feet that would leave most men self-conscious, rounded off his look almost too perfectly.

When he finally reached us, my smile broadened – again, involuntarily. His jade green eyes were striking. 'Oh Lord, I feel the poet inside of me awaken.' I imagined different shades of mosaics that were the glow of crystalline waters. I looked a little closer and couldn't help but compare them to someone who had been crying for far too long, allowing the color to run and smudge into the white of his eyes. Beautiful and sensual eyes, complemented by his otherwise dark looks. He was sun-tanned, muscular, tall and I was convinced, a little on the rough side.

'Oh my.'

My heart skipped a beat as those Daniel-butterflies began to awaken again. When he smiled at my father, my stomach turned, and I lifted my leg slightly to the back of me.

'Why do I do that?'

"Hey Ryan. How you man?"

"Good, good, thank you, Mr. Channing."

After shaking this cowboy's hand, my dad turned to me,

I DO (NOT) – AT THE RODEO

"This is my daughter, Ally. She's visiting from Willow County."

He reached out for my hand, and when I placed my hand in his, I couldn't otherwise, but stare. Shamelessly. They must have been the largest hands I had ever seen. Rough. Strong. Tanned. Firm. Enormous. Did I mention strong?

He shook my hand, and I realized at once that he had no clue of how much strength he carried in those hands. It almost hurt.

"Nice to meet you ma'am. Ryan. Henderson. But you can call me Ray."

"Ray?"

I didn't want to let go of his hand and was at once intrigued by this striking, larger than life and gorgeous cowboy.

There was not one specific feature I could pinpoint that made him handsome, although his eyes came damn close. He was the whole package and I could tell at once; a genuine, to the bone kind of cowboy.

"My friends call me Ray after my dad misspelled my name on my birth certificate. Legally, I am Rayn instead of Ryan."

I giggled unexpectedly. His sense of humor almost blew me away. There was something about his voice and accent that radiated a kind of warmth I hadn't felt in a long time. He let go of my hand, lifted his hat somewhat, bowed slightly and smiled before he turned back to my father, "I was hoping you'd let us have the use of two of Miss Sylvia's horses for a children's rope-throwing contest tomorrow?

"Sure. Do you only need two?"

"Yes sir. Just two will suffice."

Suffice. This cowboy used the word suffice. Hmm. I liked that and mixed in with his accent, I was slightly bowled over. I knew for a fact that I was grinning from ear to ear. I didn't care.

"Sure, Ally will bring them over. I presume to the bull rink?"

He nodded and thanked my dad, smiled again before he turned back to me,

"I would appreciate that, ma'am."

I was suddenly shy. I reached for a strand of hair and put it in my mouth before I began swaying from side to side.

'Stop it, Ally. Why do I do that?'

"It would be a pleasure. What time?"

"Around ten, ma'am."

I nodded and swung all at the same time. I was pretty sure I left him with the impression of the loser I was in high school.

"I better be off, the eight-seconds are about to begin."

'Yummy!' Take note, I did not say 'nice.'

Before Ray or Ryan or whatever his name was turned to

walk away, I noticed his buckle. Yes, I looked! But, with all my gaping and gawking, my eyes would not trail past that damn buckle.

'RH.'

There was nothing more appealing to me at that very moment than imagining that rodeo 'pride' that had to be forcefully held back by a buckle. I drooled. Blatantly.

When Ryan walked away, I stared at his posture as he hurriedly made his way back to the rodeo. I was hopelessly fixated on his rear and equally muscular legs. His shoulders were broad, his back was curved and mighty. I was lost. All I could think of was that undressed body on top of me, under me, or next to me. Whatever. As long as it was against me.

'Ally Bradshaw!'

'Oh, zip it! I am going to make that cowboy mine for the night.' My inner struggle had begun. My demons had come out to play. My body sided with the demons and there was no fighting them. There was no controlling them. I was powerless, and my good sense was gone. Lost. Missing.

"Are you alright here, dad? I don't want to miss the eight-second men ... uhm ... rodeo?"

Thankfully, my dad was preoccupied with one of the horses and I was quite sure he didn't catch my slip-up.

"Sure honey ... do you plan on staying for the barn dance tonight?"

I DO (NOT) – AT THE RODEO

"I'd like to?"

"Alright. We'll be leaving when it starts, but you are welcomed to call me when you're ready to be picked up."

"Thanks dad. Shout if you need me, okay?"

He nodded his head before I turned away to follow that mighty cowboy to the rodeo.

When I reached the pavilion looking down on the bull rink, hundreds of spectators had already taken their seats. I shuffled through the crowds as I swiftly made my way down. I wanted to get as close as I possibly could. I glanced around me but couldn't see Ryan anywhere. In the second row, I spotted an empty seat and quickly slipped into it when spectators began cheering excitedly in anticipation of the upcoming eight-second rodeo riders.

When the first bull came out, I clapped my hands and jumped to my feet in anticipation of the first eight-second cowboy. It was not Ryan, but I was equally excited to watch him go through eight seconds of bull riding.

The bull he was on was fierce and ruthless, and cowboy number one could hardly make it to four seconds before he was thrown. A horse was sent in to distract the bull while cowboy number one was helped to his feet by two other cowboys and what appeared to be a bull-fighter.

'Oooh. There he is.'

I immediately spotted Ryan when he walked cowboy number one out through the gate. The crowd began to cheer again when the next bull entered the rink with cowboy number two. This time, it was barely two seconds before it was over.

'Oh Lord. Where are the real cowboys?'

Again, Ryan accompanied number two out of the bull rink. When cowboy number three came into the rink, I stood up again. This time, it was Ryan. I hoped he made his eight seconds; I would hate to be put off by a cowboy simply because of his inability to cling to a bull for eight seconds. I was slightly disgusted by the other two and knew how put off Ryan I'd be. I wanted an achiever. Preferably, an over-achiever but I was not betting on it.

'You're such a judgmental bitch, Ally Bradshaw. I know.'

The bull began to kick and jump violently the moment it entered the rink. Ryan held on with one hand and swung his other arm into the air. I watched him closely. It reminded me of my dad when I used to gaze at him from that very same pavilion. I watched Ryan's muscular arm swing wildly as his body synchronized perfectly with the bull who was making desperate attempts to throw him.

Ryan held on as they went around in circles and as the bull continued to buck with all the strength it could muster up. 'Almost there'. When the alarm finally sounded, I jumped up and down in ecstasy and applauded frantically. It was the longest eight seconds of my life.

I whistled loudly and through sheer excitement, I brazenly shouted out to him, "Whooo hoooo cowboy!"

Alice VL

I DO (NOT) – AT THE RODEO

A horse trotted into the rink and grabbed Ryan from the bull. As they turned to leave, he looked up and raised his hat to the crowd before he bowed his head. Ryan was indeed, the first eight-second winner for the day. When he spotted me in the crowd, his eyes fixed a gaze on mine. I waved and smile and couldn't help but throw out another,

"Whooo hoooo!"

The entire crowd began to cheer wildly, but Ryan stared and smiled broadly at me with an unmistakable look of pride on his face. When he disappeared through a gate and into a tunnel, I took my seat again and waited for the next eight-second cowboy to fearlessly take on that savage of a bull.

For the next hour, I sat and excitedly watched another dozen or so cowboys attempt their eight seconds on a number of fearless bulls. Another two made it through to eight seconds, but none of them as sensual or erotic as Ryan did. To me, anyway.

"Howdy."

I was instantly aware of a presence behind me and when I turned to look up, a giant of a cowboy was towering over me. It was Ryan.

"Hi."

'Eight-second cowboy, hello!'

"So, the rodeo's over …"

"Yeah, I'm just waiting for the crowd to clear out. I hate crowds and the pushing and shoving that goes with it."

I DO (NOT) – AT THE RODEO

"Do you want me to sit with you?"

"Sure."

I shifted only slightly, but enough for him to take a seat next to me. I smiled and was pleasantly introduced to his overwhelming scent. At last. A scent.

'Now that's more like it.'

I couldn't quite place my finger on it but something about Ryan's odor reminded me of freshly cut timber. Perhaps a combination of pine and honey. I couldn't quite decide if it was sandalwood or honey-suckle. I liked it. I closed my eyes and breathed him in. Without a fraction of a doubt, I knew at that very second, that this cowboy was going to be trouble.

"So, will I be seeing you at the barn dance?"

"Yep. It begins in an hour, right?"

"The moment the sun has gone down."

I smiled and nodded. The more things changed, the more they stayed exactly the same. There was never a time or era, or as much as a moment to anything in Water Hills. It was always only about the sun; when it rises, and when it sets.

When the crowd finally cleared out of the pavilion, I stood up and turned my back to the setting sun.

"I better go …"

Ryan rose to his feet and again, I noticed how he towered over me. I gazed dreamily into his emerald green eyes and was at

Alice VL

once, obsessed with the look on his face. He seemed a little out of place, and edgy. He anxiously took my hand and gently squeezed it. Again, this eight-second cowboy underestimated his strength.

"I'll see you later?"

"You bet."

I smiled the sweetest smile I could conjure up from deep inside of me; the cutest, most proper Southern smile I could muster up when all I wanted to do was seduce him.

I DO (NOT) – AT THE RODEO

When I reached my mom's stand, my dad had already begun helping her pack up for the night. I turned to him and cautiously touched his arm,

"My bag is in the truck ... can I go and get it before you guys drive off with it?"

My father looked up at me and smiled. My mother glared over in our direction and frowned,

"Leave it there, we're all leaving any minute now anyway, Ally ..." My mom shot a sharp look at me.

"Oh, Ally is staying for the barn dance."

My dad blurted out before I could interrupt or say a word.

"Well, how will she get home?"

"I'll call dad when I'm ready to come home, mom."

My dad quickly grabbed the keys from his pocket and handed them over to me. I couldn't get away from my mother's stare quick enough and hurriedly made my way over to where the truck was parked.

I grabbed my bag and pulled out my mobile phone. When I noticed a flickering light, I quickly scrolled down to my messages. A message from Daniel. Again, my stomach churns. Again, my emotions unnerve me.

'Having fun? I hope you miss me just a little?'

Smiling had become my favorite thing to do when I heard

I DO (NOT) – AT THE RODEO

Daniel's voice or each time he texted me. It reminded me in no uncertain terms that he was back home, thinking of me. It gently nudged me and told me that he felt like home to me and that he was waiting for me. Somewhere, a few hundred miles from Water Hills was a fireman, sitting at home and thinking of Ally Bradshaw.

'My first day. Let's see how that goes. On my way to the first barn dance of the season.'

Within seconds, Daniel replied,

'Good Lord. Have you already found your next victim?'

I cringed when Daniel referred to my good-time, fun-loving and newly-acquainted friends who I was willing to conquer, as victims.

'Victim?'

'Why must he refer to them as victims?' I hit send and without waiting for a response, I swiftly made my way back to my parents. When I handed my father back his keys, I kissed him on his cheek,

"I'll call you, okay?"

My dad lovingly hugged me before he placed his keys back in his pocket.

"See you later mom."

She didn't look at me and without responding or acknowledging me, she carried on packing up what was left of the pies and cakes. My heart sank to my feet. I didn't understand my mother's anger towards me. I couldn't quite figure out why I disgusted her so much. I turned away still holding my mobile phone in my hand and when I glanced down, and noticed a new message from Daniel,

'Be careful.'

'Thanks, Danny.

This time, I smiled when I hit send and slowly made my way down to the barn. The barn had been used for proms, barn dances, weddings, receptions and birthday parties ever since I could remember. It was the same barn I had celebrated my eighteenth birth in and the same one Max celebrated his eighteenth in.

It was built against the river, and I could remember Church picnics and baptisms being held there. It was beautiful and when the sun began to set over the river, I gazed out into the distance and thought of Daniel. 'He would love this.'

"You made it."

I was at once yanked back to reality and when I turned around, Ryan was standing behind me.

'Damn, he is one hot, eight-second cowboy.'

All I could do was smile,

"I forgot how beautiful it is out here ... how come I've never met you before?" I was intrigued, and wanted to know all I could about Ryan.

Alice VL

I DO (NOT) – AT THE RODEO

"Oh, we bought the farm next to yours when old man Price died last year. We haven't been here that long."

"Oh right ... makes sense. You should be very happy here. This place is great."

"Yeah ..."

Ryan sat down on the grass and gazed dreamily out over the river. I anxiously sat down beside him and could once again, hardly ignore his magnificent scent.

"So, how long are you here for Ally?"

"Three weeks ... give or take; if I don't lose my mind in the meantime ..."

He nodded and smiled before he turned to face me,

"You probably have a boyfriend or a husband, or a girl friend or a wife back home?"

I giggled again. A wife or a girlfriend?

"No. I am divorced. Recently."

He frowned, and I couldn't quite make out whether he was slightly disappointed that I was divorced, or that I was even married to begin with?

"Sorry to hear."

"Oh no. don't be. I'm not. He's actually the reason I'm here. Michael comes from Water Hills too and is just as much of a jerk as most people here are. He is a dick."

Alice VL

I DO (NOT) – AT THE RODEO

'Oh Lord. Did I just say that out loud?'

Ryan chuckled and turned his head back to the river,

"You?"

"Me what?"

"Girlfriend … wife? Boyfriend … husband?"

He burst out laughing and lifted his legs until his knees touched his chin. This man was a giant. Gentle, but still a giant.

"Nah. I am too busy on the farm for romance."

"Wait. You live alone on that farm?"

"No, my mom lives with me. My dad passed away when I was ten years old. I figured I bring her out here with me and start over."

"That's sweet."

"Yeah. She lives in a cottage on the farm lands. We clash way more than is normal, but at least we're not in each other's faces all the time. She does her own thing, and I do mine."

"Yeah. I know what you mean."

"Really? Your parents are remarkable people."

"My dad is fine, although … he never used to be like this. I am still feeling him out, but my mom and I … we just don't see eye to eye. On anything."

"That sucks."

I DO (NOT) – AT THE RODEO

"Yep. I get the feeling she loves Michael more than she loves me."

Ryan frowned and stared questioningly at me,

"Michael ... my ex-husband."

"Oh, right."

"I mean ... he cheated on me with my best friend and my mom will still find a way to turn that into my fault."

'Why am I telling him this?'

"Oh man. What a dick."

"Right?"

I like this cowboy. A lot. He got up from the grass and held his hand out to me.

"Shall we go in?"

When I took his hand, he gently pulled me up to my feet. Strong. So, so strong. I couldn't quite figure out how I was going to land this one. I got the feeling that he wasn't an easy catch, but I was committed to try. After all, hasn't it become a little bit about the hunt?

Still holding his hand, I followed him into the barn. There were hundreds, more accurately, around two hundred youngsters and people my age dancing, drinking and eating. The music was deafening, but the vibe was fabulous and energetic. Just like I remembered. The barn was filled with lights that competed grandly with the Northern Lights. I could barely see the

Alice VL

dance floor beneath all the feet dancing as though they were back in the 60's somewhere.

"Ally Channing!"

I heard a sharp, chilling voice call out to me.

When I noticed a tiny, petite little frame of a person run up to me, I immediately recognized her as Heather Sheffield, Max's girlfriend. When he was still alive.

I was at once horrified. Saddened. Angry. Unnerved. I glanced down at her belly and noticed how very pregnant she was. Hugely pregnant. My heart shattered into a million pieces for Max. I could feel the tears flicker in my eyes and was instantly enraged at Heather for landing herself in such a position and blatantly moving on after Max.

'How dare she?'

"Heather?"

When she reached me, she flung her arms around me and held me against her for an awkward moment too long. I hugged her back and was secretly glad to see her; the last connection to Max. I was not happy that she was pregnant, and I was hugely disappointed that she had found someone new and that Max was finally, nothing more than someone she used to know.

'How dare she?'

"It's so good to see you!"

I DO (NOT) – AT THE RODEO

"It's good to see you too, Heather. Congratulations?"

"Thank you, Ally. Really. So, what brings you here?"

"My parents."

She leaned in closer, ready to whisper in my ear. Ryan was staring at us, listening attentively,

"I heard about you drugging and raping Michael …"

I was shocked. Disgusted. Appalled. Embarrassed. Ashamed. And while filtering through my strangling emotions, I didn't quite know how to respond.

"Heather? I don't know where you get that, but that is most certainly not how it happened."

Ryan chuckled softly before he squeezed my hand and finally, erupted into a fit of laughter. In all honesty, I knew that he was desperate to keep it in, but he failed miserably. I could see him hold back and swallow back his laughter, unfortunately, he managed it for only so long before he caved in and surrendered.

It was not so much what Heather had said, but more, the way she said it.

"Whatever you say, Ally."

"Yes, Heather, that is exactly what I'm saying. Think what you like. Whatever, I don't care. And while you're standing here trying to figure it all out, I'll be over there, dancing." I pointed to the dance floor before I immediately turned my back on her.

Alice VL

Ryan pulled me towards him and walked off, dragging me behind him, all at the same time.

I was mortified. Disgraced. Disarmed. I was horrified.

I glanced shamefacedly over at Ryan who was laughing so loudly, he could hardly walk straight,

"I'm sorry, Ally. I'm not laughing at the drugging and raping part. It's just … you should have seen your face."

"That's not what happened."

"Let's get you a drink and you can tell me all about it."

"I don't want to."

We marched over to the bar, and when we reached the barman waiting to take Ryan's order, he turned back to me,

"What's your poison."

'You.' I was so tempted to say it out loud but instead, I behaved myself. I was still utterly caught off-guard by Heather's unfounded statement and accusatory tone.

"I'll have a beer, thanks."

Ryan did his best to wipe the grin off his face before he turned back to the bar tender,

"Two beers please."

When the barman handed him the beers, he offered one to me and stared at me again.

Alice VL

I DO (NOT) – AT THE RODEO

"I didn't drug him, and I didn't rape him. I simply blindfolded him, tied him up and called his girlfriend … with an exposed … uhm … well, you know?"

Ryan tilted his head back and burst out laughing again. When he finally looked back at me, he gulped down slightly more than half his beer. The tears were glistening in his eyes as he desperately tried to control his laughter. I shook my head and sipped on my beer. Like the lady, I am.

"Who cares, Ally? It's none of any of these folk's business. So, what if you did? People are going to say what they say whether it is the truth or not. I wouldn't worry too much …"

I nodded my head, but I was still outraged by Heather's frankness. I wished I could just shut her up. The bitch.

"She used to date my brother before he died. Heather. I never thought she was good enough for him, but he loved her, so I just tolerated her for his and my parents' sake."

"The heart wants what the heart wants."

I sipped on my beer again,

"Now she's pregnant. I don't know how she can do that to my brother."

He placed his beer on the bar counter and turned back to me.

"Ally, your brother has been gone for sixteen years … surely you don't expect Heather to pine for him forever? Sixteen years is a long time …"

Alice VL

I DO (NOT) – AT THE RODEO

"You know about Max?"

"Our rope-throwing event is in honor of your brother. Everyone knows who Max Channing is. He died champion of the Water Hills rope-throwing events. He is a legend and it's an honor to have you here tomorrow, representing him."

My heart dropped. I could almost hear it shatter into a million tiny pieces. It still hurt. I was sad, and it showed.

"Thank you for that. Thank you for remembering my brother."

Ryan took my beer from me and placed it on the counter next to his, before he took my hand firmly into his,

"Come on, let's go dance."

I didn't protest and when we reached the dance floor, he placed his arms around my waist and pressed me firmly against him.

"I honestly think that you don't know how strong you are … you underestimate yourself …"

I slid my arms around his neck and smiled up at him.

"I'm sorry."

"Don't be. I like strong men."

The song ended just as we had begun to slow dance. I was disappointed, but moments later, I heard Reba McEntire's voice echo throughout the barn. 'Can I get any luckier?'

Alice VL

I DO (NOT) – AT THE RODEO

Ryan pulled me closer before I rested my head against his chest. I tried to imagine what he looked like under that blue-checked shirt. His odor was terrific. Mind-altering. But, he didn't smell or feel like Daniel. Nobody feels like Daniel.

'Forget. Daniel. Ally. Bradshaw.'

When Ryan tightened his grip around me, I closed my eyes. Again, I could smell him and I breathed him in, wanting his scent to linger for as long as it could. The warmth of his body wholly drew me in, and held me there as though I was frozen in the moment.

'Focus, Ally.'

When the song ended, I looked up at him and was taken aback when I noticed him staring at me.

"Let's get out of here."

He winked shyly before I smiled and grabbed his hand. We stopped by the bar to grab our beers before he led me back out to the river.

We strolled along the riverside in silence until we reached the stables. The horses had been closed in for the night. It was quiet. It was dark with only a paraffin lantern burning at the entrance of the stables.

Ryan made his way over to a bale of hay and sat down, sipping on his beer. I gulped down what was left of mine and placed the bottle down on the floor below me.

Ryan removed his hat and for the first time since I met

him, I could clearly identify his devilish good looks. He had beautiful hair, almost too gorgeous for a cowboy. There was no doubt in my mind that his hair magnified the color of his striking eyes.

There was no denying that this eight-second cowboy had gotten me in a twist. Every inch of me was on alert and my body let me know that it clammily approved. Clammily? This cowboy was making me lose all sense, intelligence and the sanctity of words as I discovered a whole new kind of language with terms I had never heard of before; that simply didn't exist. Clammily?

I walked up to him and came to a halt right in front of him. I didn't want to make my intentions too obvious at that very moment, and I hoped he would make the first move. When he stood up, he slowly, but nervously removed my sweater.

'Touch down!'

With a hammering heart, I turned around and lifted my hair that was flowing loosely down my back. I hoped by exposing my zipper, I would send the message I was trying to convey and get out to him.

He slowly unzipped me and turned me around to face him. When my dress fell to the ground, he finally removed his blue-checked shirt. I was like a kid in a toy-store and couldn't wait to discover all that was hiding underneath.

'Ally bloody Bradshaw.'

I was not disappointed. At all. He looked even better than I could ever have imagined or dreamed up. In a thousand years, I could never have quite pictured how flawlessly carved, smooth and chiseled his chest was. 'I want to see more.' I inhaled sharply and stared brazenly at his shirtless torso. He was sculptured to perfection with a popping six-pack.

This cowboy's biceps were the size of footballs. His round and protruding shoulders added so much more flavor to his already flawless physique. I wanted to touch him. I wanted to run my fingers through every dent, and each protruding muscle.

I moved closer and grabbed his buckle with all my might. To my surprise, it clipped off easily and fell to the ground. When I reached down to his crotch, I struggled with the button on his jeans, and when he began kissing me on my shoulder, I was frantic to unbutton him.

'Finally.'

I pulled the zipper down and was slightly disappointed to discover tight-fitting, restricting Jockeys underneath. Confining and limiting. I could feel him shift awkwardly but I couldn't stop myself from beaming, from ear to ear.

Ryan lowered his Jockeys until he was finally freed and exposed. With a fuzziness and a slight blur in front of my eyes, I took a moment to absorb and appreciate the physique of a man, one I compared to soft, imported Italian silk hiding behind the hardened, cowboy appearance. While exploring every inch of him, he stirred somewhat and again, shift uncomfortably right before my eyes.

He presented himself like someone or something I had never seen before. Perfect. Another work of art, but what was right before my eyes was more than that; it was exquisite and rare. I blushed and gazed at him, and like a rock star fan meeting her idle for the very first time, I flagrantly admired the stature of a man that was standing so close to me. I could almost see the murky puddles in his eyes seep out into mine.

I moved closer and slowly trailed down his body with my mouth. My lips were slightly swollen as it desperately made its way down his eight-second frame. I stood up again when I felt his body become rigid. I kissed him delicately, desperate to taste him and was pleasantly surprised that he tasted of honey. His breath was warm and his lips were entirely bewitching. I could stand there kissing him, and do nothing else.

I was entirely swept up in the moment and had no plans of surrendering to him just yet, when Ryan pressed me securely against him and swept me up into his arms. He turned around and laid me down on a bale of hay.

He lowered himself delicately on top of me, resting the full force of his weight on his elbows as he began to slice into my body with his mouth. My breaths became shallow and shaky as he embarked on a mission to explore my entire body with only his mouth. I closed my eyes when he reached my thighs, realizing that my senses were instantly awakened and seduced.

My legs began to shudder slightly when he lingered for only a moment before he made his way back up and kissed me passionately. With his elbows at my sides, he pulled me closer and clenched by head with both his hands.

I was confused. It was intimate and personal. Gentle. Slow. He placed a hand under me and lifted me slightly. I could feel the entire weight of his body on me and was ready for anything this cowboy was about to offer me. My heart began to race, and my breaths grew shorter.

He was nothing like the cowboy that handled that beast of a bull with strength, confidence and power. Instead, as strong and as determined he was to ride out those eight seconds, as gentle and meek he was to ride me out.

While lingering in the kiss that Ryan was sweeping me up into, my entire body erupted into one mammoth quiver. His mouth was getting the better of me.

My arms reached around him while exploring the brand-new world of a kiss that I never wanted to end. I wanted him. I wanted all of him and without ending the exquisite and passionate kiss, I wanted him there and then. As I shifted below him, trying to signal to him that I was ready, he suddenly lifted himself off me and got back onto his feet.

I was horrified. My entire body was aching and quaking. 'What now?' He bent down and picked me up before he placed me back on my feet. He turned me around and began kissing me in my neck, trailing down to my shoulder and down my back.

My body was engulfed in goosebumps and Ryan was taking his time. He was taking just a little too long for my liking and when he walked around to face me, he kissed me in my neck and slowly, he tracked his way down to the rest of my body once again.

My legs grew weak instantly and were giving in under me. When I was once again introduced to a million tiny little fluxes rushing through me, I could barely keep my legs upright.

I was fiercely shaking and bent down slightly, afraid that my legs were about to give way underneath me. I grabbed onto his hair and tried with all my strength to pull him away from me. I was growing increasingly weaker with every heavenly touch on me, and when I realized my legs would not keep me up for much longer, I tugged at him one last time.

As the build-up inside of me threatened to rupture, he finally released me. I had to catch my breath and whimpered boldly. I could barely control my body and I couldn't regulate the horrifying sounds I heard coming from my mouth.

He picked me up and when I folded my legs around him, he pressed me against him and held powerfully onto me. He held me compellingly against him and with the wall behind me, he gently pushed me against it and lifted me up slightly higher than he was.

I could no longer see much of anything in front of me. My entire body quivered and broke out into a spasm all at the same time. Not only was I at once sensitive to all the senses I had been getting to know so well, but I was alerted to uproars from an entire different angle rush throughout my body.

It was almost as though there were pressure and pleasure points I wasn't aware of until that moment; in a barn with an eight-second cowboy in my hometown.

I could barely think straight when I closed my eyes and did nothing else but surrendered exclusively to Ryan. I murmured unashamedly while I clenched tighter and tighter around him.

I DO (NOT) – AT THE RODEO

With each thrust I felt him drive with more precision and with each prod, I was aware of a brand-new rush.

My arms folded around his head as I tried to identify and predict what was coming next. I couldn't. As though each and every part of me was fitted with a speck of decadence, they all detonated at once. It was almost as a blinding flash of blue-white lights that rolled out on the skyline, followed by fists of orange flames shattering all the windows around us.

I could feel the ripples begin at the very core of me and trickle slowly into every inch of me. Like four, maybe five oceans coming together on a wild, stormy night when the waves crashed at different angles before eventually flowing into each other.

Like a thunderous storm sending jolts of lightning throughout my body, my legs locked around him. My body distanced itself from my mind, heart and soul and I had no clue of what I was getting myself into. Yet, I savored each sensation rushing up and down my spine, and when he pressed me a little tighter against the wall, I imagined he was feeling it too.

Like a deadly rain showering down on us, I could hear him grunt and groan. His breathing was synchronized with mine and his body was as tense and sweaty as mine. He suddenly pulled me away from the wall and pressed me firmly against him. Out of nowhere, he stopped, as though to estimate the damage the fire, lighting and rain had brought down on us.

I didn't want to come down from the magnificent high my eight-second cowboy placed me on. I didn't want to be stopped by any number of missiles that would strike, leaving clouds of smoke around us. This cowboy was trouble. Deep

Alice VL

trouble. Beautiful, gratifying, sensual and addictive trouble.

My body was still trembling slightly when he placed me down on my feet. I was shocked. Stunned. In awe of him. I felt fuzzy and shaky and my legs still didn't quite want to keep me up and continued to quiver violently.

He smiled reservedly at me before he picked up my dress from the floor and handed it back to me,

"Your dress, ma'am."

Taking my dress from him, I could still hear myself panting breathlessly. But, I was not the only one. Ryan-Ray was still wheezing too.

I slipped my dress on over my head and made a valiant attempt to stand firmly on my trembling feet. Ryan walked around behind me and zipped up my dress before he kissed me in my neck again. My sweater was on the floor below me, and when I threw it over me, he walked over to a bale of hay. He shook out his blue-checked shirt and placed it neatly on the hay before he turned back to me, signaling for me to take a seat.

"Shall we go back to the dance or do you want to sit here for a minute?"

I walked over to him and sat down sluggishly. I was still dazed and totally speechless. How was it possible that he could be so cool, calm and collected after I had just crossed a million portals for an earth-shattering encounter? One I had truly never had before. One, I would never dare try and explain or expect to experience again. "No ... let's just sit here for a while ..."

I DO (NOT) – AT THE RODEO

"You alright?"

He sat down beside me and took my hand into his. Staring at our hands intertwined like that, I looked up at him and smiled. I could just imagine what I looked like. My cheeks were without a doubt flustered, and my hair must have been a hot mess. When he pulled out a straw of hay from my hair and smiled, I knew I looked like chaos.

"I'm fine. You are trouble, Ryan."

"What cowboy isn't?"

I chortled softly and for an instant, I didn't know what to say next.

"You seduced me, Ally Bradshaw."

"I did no such thing …"

We both burst out laughing and I couldn't help but think back to the Ally of a year ago who would never be caught dead in a barn, cavorting with a cowboy surrounded by hay.

"I have to go … my parents …"

"Can I drive you?"

'No. No. No.' I jumped to my feet, frantic to excuse myself and make a call to my father,

"No, I'll give my dad a call."

"Ally Bradshaw. I may be a cowboy, but I am a gentleman too. I will drive you home. My mama raised a cowboy with manners."

How on earth could I ever deny him his right as a gentleman? A cowboy gentleman. I wasn't there to strip any man of his masculinity. Except Michael.

"Alright."

I DO (NOT) – AT THE RODEO

I strolled into the farmhouse a few minutes after midnight. It was dark and quiet and as softly as I possibly could, I opened the front door and tiptoed into my parents' house careful not to make a sound. 'Why do I feel like a teenager sneaking back into my parents' home?'

I shut the front door without making as much as a peep and when I turned around, I turned smack-bang into my mother who was standing behind me with her hands on her hips. My heart dropped at once. She had just given me the fright of my life.

"Ally Bradshaw … do you know what time it is? Why didn't you call your father to pick you up? Who brought you home?"

"Sheez mama … you scared the shit out of me. Ryan Henderson brought me home. Do you have any idea how scary you look standing there?"

"Listen to you. Since when do you speak like that? Never mind, I've made an appointment with Reverend Carmichael for us in the morning."

I was about to protest when my dad appeared from around the corner,

"Syl … tomorrow is no good. She's taking the horses over to the rope-throwing contest."

"I told you Jason. I told you well in advance that Reverend Carmichael is coming over tomorrow."

I couldn't say for sure, but I was pretty sure my mouth hung open as I stood staring at my father. 'Is this really my dad?'

Alice VL

I DO (NOT) – AT THE RODEO

"Well, you are just going to have to re-schedule. Ally can't back out of the commitments I made for the rope-throwing contest. You know it is held in Max's honor, and Ally volunteered to represent him at the competition."

My dad was lying for me? My mom turned around and hurried back upstairs. Her annoyance and agitation was as clear as daylight. I tittered softly and turned back to my father,

"Thanks daddy."

" Come on. I have tea on the stove."

I followed my dad into the kitchen and slid into an empty chair at the kitchen table. With my bag under my chair, I gazed over at him. I was once again aware of what a giant of a man he was. His silvery hair was balding and thinning, and he had developed a slight hunch. But, what I couldn't ignore was the resigned look on his face. Like a candle's light that was slowly burning out and dying.

I was sad. Since I had come home, all I could see on his face were expressions of frustration and fatigue. I got the feeling that my dad was tired and that he had had enough of this world. I had a nagging feeling that my father was ready to leave and see Max again.

He poured our tea and handed me a cup before he slid into a chair next to me.

"So, my girl. What's going on with you?"

"Nothing dad. Honestly. I am not the person mom thinks I am or the woman Michael is making me out to be."

Alice VL

I DO (NOT) – AT THE RODEO

"You really want no future with Michael?"

"No dad. I don't love him. I don't think I ever did."

"Then why did you marry him, Ally?"

"I don't know, dad? I thought I loved him. After Max died, I just felt so alone. I lost my best friend. You and mom just sort of disappeared and I kinda felt like I lost you too. You don't know what it was like looking at the two of you every single day. You were sad all the time. Mom was angry all the time. I can remember the days she wouldn't even get out of bed, and then I can remember the days that she would blame you. I hated it. I just couldn't watch you guys anymore."

My dad sighed miserably before he took my hand and gently squeezed it,

"I'm sorry, baby. I know we checked out on you for a while."

"That's okay, dad. I don't blame you; not you or mom. I know it was hard but now, for the first time in my life, I am truly happy. I feel free. I have a great job, a beautiful home … and I have you."

I smiled and rested my head against his shoulder.

"I just don't want you to be lonely, my girl."

"I'm not lonely dad. I have friends … I see … people."

"Anyone special?"

"No … but I date, and I like meeting new people."

Alice VL

"Your mother ... she takes a while to come around. Her mind is still set on Michael."

"I know dad, but I can't stand her judging me all the time. I don't need a pastor dad ... I need my mama."

"Just give her time. She's still in there somewhere ..."

My dad looked helpless and defeated. It looked as though he had been carrying the burden of losing Max for far too long. Having to look into my mother's distraught face each day must have been cruel and exhausting for him.

I knew without a doubt that it was slowly killing him. I didn't know what to say anymore. I didn't know what to do, so instead of saying anything at all, I placed my arms around my father, and held him tightly.

"And you, dad? Are you alright. You scared me a little today and I don't know what's gotten into you? You are so laid back lately?"

He burst out laughing and frowned,

"Life is short Ally. We can't keep punishing you because Max died. I want you to live your life to the fullest. You're still young, you should go out and explore the world and do more of what makes you happy. I'm okay my darling. Don't you worry about me. Your mama does that just fine."

Finally. At thirty-one-years old, my dad finally came around. At that very second, I loved him more than ever.

"Well, I'm going to crawl in, daddy. Will you be coming to

the rope-throwing contest tomorrow?"

"Tomorrow is a busy day with the horses. I highly doubt it, but how about we meet up for lunch at mama's stall for pie or cake?"

"I'd love that, daddy."

I got up and placed my arms around my father again. He smelled of grass and rain; but more importantly, he smelled like my dad. Perhaps coming home wasn't such a bad thing after all?

When I reached my bedroom, I gazed around at all the wall posters covering my wall. It felt as though I had stepped back into my teen years and for a split-second, I wondered why my mother had never changed a thing. I thought about Max's bedroom next to mine and I wondered whether he's bedroom had been left untouched, just as mine had.

The wooden floors creaked mercilessly as I tiptoed into the bedroom next door. The door was shut, but when I turned the handle, I peeked into his bedroom, expecting to find him there. I was expecting to find him enraged by the fact that I had opened his door without knocking. How I would gladly have taken a scolding from him, just to have him back again.

It was dark, with only the light of the moon shining through his bedroom window. I walked in slowly and closed the door behind me. It was all still the same. Nothing had been touched. My heart dropped instantly when I noticed his motorbike helmet on his desk. I missed him. I so badly wanted to see my brother again and when I noticed his black leather jacket still sloped around a chair in the corner, I could feel his presence all around me.

I tiptoed over to the chair in the corner and picked it up. It smelled of cologne and it felt as though Max was in the room and standing close to me. A lump in my throat was growing and threatening to silence me. I swallowed back on the tears that were beginning to gush from my eyes and down my cheeks. It hurt. I missed him.

I was suddenly aware of a slight shuffle behind me, and when I turned around, I noticed my mother asleep on his bed. My heart hurt for her. My stomach hurt. She missed him so. She looked so sad lying there with her eyes closed. So small and helpless. I had a nagging feeling that, like my father, my mother was ready to throw in the towel, and surrender to her grief. My heart hurt was crushed and ached so badly.

I walked over to her and threw a quilt over her. I slid in beside her and wrapped an arm around her. We all missed Max. Nothing had been the same since he left.

Mama smelled like roses. I thought back to how I used to lay on her lap and fall asleep to the smell of freshly cut roses. I longed for those days. I yearned for the woman she was before Max died. I missed her loving me.

Alice VL

I DO (NOT) – AT THE RODEO

When I opened my eyes again, the sun was peering in through the windows, lighting up Max's entire bedroom. I quickly glanced over next to me, but mama was gone. I climbed out of bed and neatly folded his quilt before I laid it down at the end of his bed. Without looking back again, I quietly made my way back to my bedroom.

I reached for my mobile phone and was just about to scroll down to the messages when my mother appeared in my doorway.

"Here's a cup of coffee. Breakfast will be ready in ten minutes."

She handed me a cup of coffee and smiled sadly.

"Thank you, mom."

I sipped on the warm coffee and when she turned to leave, I had a sudden, inexplicable urge to hug my mother.

"Mom?"

She stopped and turned around at once. I walked over to her and hesitated for a second. I was not quite sure how she would react and it left me feeling insecure. I was hesitant. Afraid. Sad. I placed my arms around her and held her tightly against me.

"I miss him too, mama."

She didn't say a word. She didn't place one single arm around me. She just stood there motionlessly, and without saying a single word. When I stepped back, she sneered wretchedly and simply walked away from me.

Alice VL

I DO (NOT) – AT THE RODEO

I wished with all my heart my mother would say something. I wished I could say something to make her feel better, but it was always a case of the harder I tried, the more she would disconnect from me and disappear into her own world. One she had created to escape us, and wander around in amidst her grief. It was a world that didn't treat her well, yet she chose it above us. She chose it, because that's where Max was. That was where she felt she didn't betray him by being happy again. By living again. That was where she was drowning, one unforgiving and heartless wave at a time. I left her there. I had no way of knowing how to bring her back to us and let her know that Max would forgive her.

The flickering light on my mobile phone distracted me at once, and when I scrolled down, I was happy to discover a new message from Daniel. Not once did Daniel cross my mind while cavorting with my eight-second cowboy, and I was slightly relieved by it. Yet, seeing his name on the screen made my stomach turn, and awakened the fluttering of those damn deceitful butterflies.

'You okay?'

I smiled discontentedly. Again, I wished things were different between Daniel and I.

'Better than expected. On my way to a rope-throwing contest. But then again, it's only my second day here. You good?'

Seconds later, his response came through,

'Got a date tonight. Yay me!'

Alice VL

I DO (NOT) – AT THE RODEO

Oh Lord. Really? I did not need to hear that right then.

I was annoyed. Irritated. I couldn't stand the idea of someone else having her way with Daniel. I was resentful. A little hurt and a whole lot rejected.

Without responding to his message, I switched off my mobile phone and opened the water in the shower. I stood lifelessly as the water washed over me. I could still smell Ryan on me and I wanted only Ryan on my mind.

I cold-bloodedly pushed Daniel from my mind and was at once excited at the prospect of seeing Ryan again. 'This cowboy is trouble. I know it.'

When I reached the kitchen after a quick shower, my parents were having their breakfast surrounded by a deathly silence between them. I walked in and threw caution to the wind before I sat in an empty seat across from my mother.

"It's chilly out there, Ally. Your coat is hanging in the closet."

I was wearing a pair of jeans, a T-shirt and riding boots. My hair was tied back into a ponytail and except for lipstick and light mascara, I was wearing no make-up.

"Thanks mom."

"Max's hat is in there too. Wear it. The sun is at its worst in fall."

My heart sank at once. Max. I lowered my head and nodded. I suddenly had no appetite but did my best to finish a slice of toast, an egg and a strip of bacon. When I took the last sip of my coffee, I turned to my father,

"So, I am going to take my car today. I have to be there early. Can we still meet for lunch?"

"Looking forward to it."

I got up at once and placed my dishes in the basin before I turned around to my mother,

"See you later, mama."

My mom nodded while staring blankly ahead of her. I just couldn't figure out why she always seemed so angry at me, all the time. I just wished she would say something nice to me. Just once.

As fast as I could, I rushed out to where my car was parked and stopped dead in my tracks. It felt as though someone had taken my lungs into their hands and began squeezing them with all their might. My heart was racing at the speed of a freight train and my tears were not very far off. My mother hated me, and I didn't know why? She couldn't stand the sight of me and yet, I loved her. So much. I didn't understand.

With Max's hat in my hand, I pulled myself together and climbed into my car. The drive to the fair was a short one, and when I pulled up in front of the stables, Ryan was stacking hay right outside the stable doors.

He was such a sight for sore eyes. Again, he was dressed in jeans, this time they were older, and the frays were far more tattered than his jeans from the day before. Rippier.

Alice VL

I DO (NOT) – AT THE RODEO

'Rippier? Really Ally?' This cowboy was making me stupid.

I could barely discard a picture of myself ripping out what was left of the little strands holding them together. A picture that had formed in my mind and came out of nowhere. He was wearing a red-checked shirt, and his trademark buckle stood out like a sore thumb. His hat was different, but he was as handsome as ever.

I climbed out of my car and quickly walked over to him.

When he spotted me coming towards him, he stopped and stood up to face me,

"Good mornin' ma'am."

I chuckled nervously. His Southern accent was sexy and warm. I swooned. I drooled just a little.

"Morning cowboy."

He grinned from ear to ear before he bent down and lifted the last of the hay. He pulled off his gloves and tossed them onto the haystack.

"Let's go get 'em horses."

I nodded shyly and made my way out to the stables. I walked on over to Rusty and pointed to Tramp,

"You can take Tramp over there, I'll bring Rusty out."

He nodded in agreement, and strolled over to Tramp before placing the reins over him.

Alice VL

I DO (NOT) – AT THE RODEO

"We might as well get them ready. The saddles are over there …"

I pointed to the saddles stacked in a corner in the barn. Ryan lifted a saddle off a rail and made his way over to me. When he reached me, he gently placed the saddle over Rusty.

"I've got the girdle … I'll do it."

There was no way in the world that Ryan Henderson would think that I was a city idiot. 'I can do this. I know my stuff.' When he walked back over to the second saddle, he placed it equally gently over Tramp.

"I figure we should go for a ride to warm them up? The competition doesn't begin for another hour."

'Now that's more like it.' I turned around and smiled as though it was no big deal,

"Good idea. Shall we ride down to the river?"

"Sounds good."

He climbed onto Tramp and gripped the reins firmly into his hands. I in turn, mounted Rusty with ease and when I rested my feet in the stirrups, I was at once happy that I wore my riding boots. I fixed Max's hat on my head before I led Rusty out of the stables.

When Ryan caught up with me, we slowly began to trot through the fields, avenues of trees and down to the river. We rode in silence but appreciated the magnificent view around us. I couldn't remember when the last time was that I followed that

Alice VL

trail on horseback. When we reached the mouth of the river, Ryan slid off Tramp and tied his reins around a tree. When Tramp was securely fastened, he quickly made his way over to me and held out his arms to me.

His bulky, burly strong arms left me powerless. There was no way I was going to act like the tough cowboy's daughter I was. Instead, I fell dramatically into his arms and when he placed me on my feet, he tightened his grip around me.

"Should we talk about last night?"

"No."

"You sure?"

"Positive."

He leaned down and kissed me. I closed my eyes and savored the warmth of his mouth. There was nothing soft or scrawny about this cowboy. I was hooked. He was my new master and right then, he controlled every inch of my body.

My hunger for his body was to such an extent that I felt I might go insane in a world that suddenly seemed nothing more than whimsical to me. I inhaled deeply and once again, I was pleasantly aware of his mesmerizing scent.

Ryan retreated slightly and took his hat off. He reached for mine and placed them both on the ground below us.

"I think it's a great day for a swim.'

Ryan winked slyly as he started unbuttoning his shirt.

Alice VL

I DO (NOT) – AT THE RODEO

"Swim? Are you nuts? It's fall."

"Isn't it a hot, sunny day?"

"Yeah, I guess, but I have nothing to swim in?"

"Since when do you need anything to swim in."

When the last piece of clothing was stripped from Ryan, he turned around and ran right up to the edge of the river before he dove in. I was shocked and could just guess how cold the water was. When he finally resurfaced, he turned back to a fully-dressed me,

"Ally Bradshaw. I thought you were fearless?"

"Who told you that?"

'What the hell?'' I began stripping right there at the edge of the river, more so to prove to Ryan that I was in fact, fearless. I wasn't really but when the last of my garments fell to the ground, I walked slowly and completely uncovered to the edge of the river. Like the lady I still am, I stepped into the water. It was cold, but not as cold as I thought it would be. I was instantly met by goosebumps that spread throughout my entire body. It was still damn cold.

When my body finally adjusted to the cold and the water's temperature, I swam out to Ryan and when I reached him, he instantly swept me up and into his arms.

I folded my legs around him before he gently kissed me and placed his arms firmly around me. I took his face into my icy cold and wet hands, and kissed him back fiercely.

Alice VL

I DO (NOT) – AT THE RODEO

In a split second, his warm touch piercing through the coldness of my skin touched every nerve in my body while charging the inner core of me all at once.

Again, something was altered. Different. When his hand reached around my neck and he touched my hair, the coldness of the water had made way for the warmth of his touch. I couldn't help but notice how perfectly our bodies fit together while we were submerged in the water. It was as if our bodies were perfectly synchronized with one another as it moved together like a natural rhythm. We locked eyes for just a moment before I kissed him again. I was besotted with that cowboy's mouth.

I felt my legs begin to shudder but they didn't feel like mine. It was as though they had embarked upon a life of their own, but still connected to me somehow. My hands began to quiver as though on cue, and my ability to kiss him was compromised. My breathing grew shorter and rapider when Ryan's grip on me tightened while gasping for air, yet, my lips were still not ready to leave his.

I clawed my hands into his face when my entire body began to respond and my heart began thumping in my chest. Like lightning striking down on the water around us, I was once again aware of tiny bursts of shockwaves rushing through my veins, and spilling over into my entire body.

As though out of nowhere and without warning, I was blasted into what I compared to a frenzy of static. There was no warning. No build up. No slow ascending high. When my hands began to tremble, Ryan tensed up at once and shuddered in unification with me. Just as quickly as what felt like lightning came crashing down on us, it was gone.

I leaned forward slightly and kissed him again.

"You are going to be the end of me." I whispered and giggled all at the same time.

"I hope not."

When we both began to feel the cold, we swam out back to land and while still wet and dripping with water, we threw on our dry clothes, desperate to warm up again.

We rode back to the fair in silence, and when we reached the pavilion on horseback, the crowds were beginning to find their seats on the pavilion. Thankfully, we were fully dry by the time we reached the rink.

I was slightly embarrassed and was once again convinced that the world around me knew exactly what I had been up to. Ryan smiled, almost as though he knew what I was thinking,

"Shall we go?"

"Yep. I'll follow you."

Taking Rusty's reins, I followed Ryan out to the rink. When the competition kicked off, I quickly found an empty seat amongst the hundreds of cheering spectators. Children from as young as four years old were participating and it made me think of Max again. I admired his courage when he, from a very young age, wanted to follow in our dad's footsteps. Watching the young boys below, I couldn't help but admire their bravery but more than that, I wholly approved of Ryan's way in which he coached them. I smiled often and thought of Max and how proud he would have been that the competition was in honor of him. Max loved children, and couldn't wait to settle down and start a family someday. How I wished he could see the happy faces all around us that day, and for him.

When the competition was finally over, I quickly ran down the pavilion into the rink to where Ryan was holding both Rusty and Tramp's reins.

"I better get them back."

"I'll come with you …"

"That's alright. I've got this."

I took the reins from him and turned to lead them back to the open fields where my father kept the other horses.

"Will I see you again later?"

"Maybe …"

I sneered flippantly,

'I curse this eight-second cowboy.'

When I arrived for my lunch date with my dad, my mom had the table set and was ready to serve us pie and coffee. My dad pulled out a garden chair for her and sat down on another one beside her. I took my plate and sat down on the grass next to my father.

"I think a beer is in order … don't you?"

Alice VL

I DO (NOT) – AT THE RODEO

He winked at me and handed me a beer. My eyes trailed over to my mother who was glaring at us both.

"Thanks dad."

We ate pie and drank beer in silence, while watching children as they came and went. They were strolling through the fields with the horses, feeding them the apples and carrots my dad had left out for them. I missed the way of life in Water Hills. I missed being there, like that.

For the remainder of the day, I stayed close to my dad. Together, we rode across the fields and entertained the children on horseback. My mother sold her pies and cakes, but rarely left her stall.

We arrived back at the farmhouse shortly before nine that evening. After an awkward and far too quiet dinner, my father sat out on the porch smoking a last cigarette before turning in for the night. My mother took pre-baked pies from the freezer and left them out to defrost for the next day's sales before she excused herself,

"I am off to bed. Sleep well."

I nodded and joined my father on the porch.

"I don't know how you can live with her?"

It slipped out. I didn't mean to sound so cold, but at the same time, I couldn't understand my mother's bitterness.

"Ally Bradshaw!"

Alice VL

I DO (NOT) – AT THE RODEO

"I'm sorry, dad. I mean, it's not like you're staying together for the sake of the kids?"

He turned around to face me and took my hands decisively into his. He lowered his head before squeezing them gently.

"She's my wife. For better and for worse."

"But she's so miserable, dad?"

"She never used to be like this, Ally. Life has given her a couple of hard knocks. You only know about Max; you have no idea what your mother has been through in her life."

"That's no excuse, dad. We've all been knocked off our feet and we are all still mourning Max, but we don't treat her like this."

"I know, Ally, but I love her. I still see a seventeen-year-old girl standing in front of me each time she walks into the room. My heart still does a turn around when I see your mother. With all my heart, I love her and will keep my promise to her."

I couldn't think of anything to say, instead, I just sighed. I felt sorry for my dad and then, I became angry with my mother.

"You shouldn't be so hard on her, Ally. She loves you and only wants the best for you."

"No dad. She loved Max. She still loves him so much. I sometimes wish it was me in that car that day."

My dad looked up and took my face into his hands. It

wasn't hard to notice the tears sparkle brightly in his eyes, before my own began to roll down my cheeks.

"It's not your fault, Ally. It's not your fault that you're still here and Max isn't. If it were you, your mother would be equally devastated and walk around just as she does now. She doesn't love Max more than she loves you, she loves you both equally, but differently. Is that what you think? That she would trade you for Max?"

"I know she loves me, dad. She just doesn't like me much."

"No, my girl. You've got it all wrong. She grieves both her children. When last have you come home for a visit?"

"But dad, that's because I don't want to come here. I don't want to be around her. When Michael betrayed me, I was crushed, dad. I was so hurt. I had lost twelve years of my life that I handed over to him. I was miserable and unhappy; and all I wanted was to earn Michael's love. He still chose someone else over me. I couldn't speak to mama. I couldn't tell her that my heart was broken. She just never, ever gave me the benefit of the doubt."

Not wanting my dad to see me cry, I hurriedly swabbed at the tears that were beginning to blind me. When I turned around, I noticed my mother standing in the doorway,

'How much did she hear?'

"Mama?"

"Ally … I didn't know you felt that way about me?"

Alice VL

I DO (NOT) – AT THE RODEO

I was shocked. I didn't want her to hear me say that. Devastation overwhelmed me when I realized that she probably overheard our entire conversation. I was mortified. It was never my intention to hurt her or to make her feel worse than she already did most of the time. At the same time, her standing at the door was an opportunity to lay it all out and tell her exactly how I felt. It was overdue. It was way overdue.

"Well, you know what mom? I am sorry you heard that, but at the same time, I am tired of living up to your expectations. I am tired of pretending to be the good daughter. I am tired of walking on eggshells around you. I am sick to death of how you always side with Michael and never believe a word I say. But guess what, mom? I am not your good girl. I am not your good anything. Do you know what I've been up to these last couple of months?"

Telling her that I had evolved from one extreme to the next was most certainly not appropriate, but I didn't care anymore. I paused to take in a deep breath and when I exhaled, a floodgate of tears was about to burst out inside of me. I was angry. I was crushed.

"I have been sleeping with men I don't know, and I like it! And you know what else, for the first time in my life, I am free, in control and I mean something to this world!"

My father instantly leapt to his feet. The shocked expression on his face was unnerving, but my mother did nothing more than stare blankly at me before she disappeared back into the house.

"You will not speak like that Ally!"

Alice VL

I DO (NOT) – AT THE RODEO

I turned around to look my father squarely in the eye, still desperate to hide my tears from him,

"Yes dad. I will. I will say it how it is. I am sick and tired of having to mark my words and sugarcoat everything I say. I am tired of placing filters in front of my mouth. I am not the Ally Channing you think I am and I don't care!"

He stood staring at me in silence. Not a word. Not a single sound came from his mouth in the minutes that followed my outburst. There was nothing left to say, so I turned around and ran down the porch steps.

I had to get away from them. It was only my second night home and already, I could hardly breathe. My parents were smothering me with their unrealistic expectations. I was a thirty-one-year-old grown woman; why did they have such a powerful hold over me?

I ran as fast as I could into the night. I ran through the fields and the trees until my legs could no longer carry me. I stopped dead in my tracks and leaned forward, gasping for breath. Holding onto a tree for support, I slid down, and leaned against it. I was tired. My heart hurt. My soul cried.

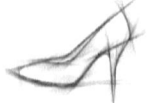

Alice VL

PART 3

When I was no longer fighting to take in a breath of fresh air, I looked up and noticed the lights burning in a farmhouse in the distance. I recognized the old farmhouse as old man Price's place. Now Ryan's home.

I got up and slowly walked over through the fields and to his home. I wanted to see a friendly face. I wanted to see Ryan. I just wanted someone to sit with, without judgements or disappointments. When I reached his front door, I hesitated for a moment.

My eyes closed instinctively as I considered my actions for a second. Daniel was on my mind. Daniel was who I wanted to see. Daniel's arms were the arms I wanted around me. I turned away at once and when I reached the bottom step of the porch, I unexpectedly heard Ryan's voice behind me,

"Ally?"

I was a total mess.

"Hey …"

"Everything alright?"

"Yep. I couldn't sleep …"

I DO (NOT) – AT THE RODEO

"Do you want to come inside?"

"I really shouldn't. I don't know why I came here …"

He walked up to me and placed his strong, powerful arms around me,

"I want you to come inside for a while. It's cold out here."

His arms felt peacefully comforting around me, and I automatically slid my arms around him, and rested my head on his chest. It was warm, soothing and safe, but it didn't feel anything like Daniel.

'Go away, Daniel.'

"Come on … let me get you a warm mug of cocoa."

I followed him inside and when he closed the door behind me, I couldn't help but notice how country'ish everything was. It was nothing like I would expect from an eight-second cowboy. It was lived-in, homely, warm and cozy. It was as though furniture had been crammed into each room, almost like an overstocked furniture store. There were solid pieces of wood, floral lamps and a wooden coat stand in the doorway. I could only guess it was a combination of Mr. Price's pieces and some of Ryan's all thrown in together. I smiled. It felt like an escape.

Ryan had a fire burning in the living room and showed me to a seat in front of it.

"Sherry or that cocoa?"

There was something about looking at him through the

illumination of a fire burning in the background that made me weak at the knees.

"Sherry thanks."

He handed me a glass and sat down beside me.

"Do you want to talk about it?"

"No. not really. My mom and I ... we just had an explosive argument. Again."

"Your mom is a good and kind woman, Ally."

"Yeah? You don't have to live with her. Ever since Max died, she sort-of checked out and began distancing herself from my dad and I. Like she's angry with me. Or ... angry that I'm here and Max is gone."

"Oh Ally ... don't you get it? Your mom is terrified of losing you, and to distance herself from you is normal. That's what mothers do when the nest gets empty especially after she's had to live through the trauma of losing one child. She won't survive another loss ..."

'Hang on. What?'

Listening to Ryan telling me that my mom is terrified of losing me was almost ridiculous. At the same time, there was something in there that rang a bell inside of me. I frowned and realized right there that I had never thought of my mother's fears or her consequent behavior in that way before. 'How does this cowboy know so much?'

Alice VL

"What do you mean?"

"Your mother was close to Max, right?"

"Yes?"

"It almost killed her when he died. I figure, she thinks if she breaks the connection with you, it won't hurt as much when you're gone. Not necessarily die, but like when you got married and left home and now, when you're back home in the city. And to be honest, I think disconnecting from you is almost harder than having to lose you. She probably deliberately began losing you while you were still here, at home. That must be hard, Ally."

Wow. Seriously? How did I, Ally Bradshaw, never once consider any of this.

"You are one hell of a guy, Ryan. Not only one mighty cowboy, but intelligent too."

He burst out laughing before he placed his empty glass on the coffee table.

"So, you really don't have a boyfriend back in the city?"

'Daniel.' There's Daniel, but instead, I shake my head.

"Nope. I mean, there's a guy back home that I really like, but … I am not ready for a relationship. I like being able to have fun with no strings attached. I like the freedom. I like that there are no expectations or dating rules. I like that it drives my mom crazy. I just told her that, you know?"

"Are you kidding? You told your mom you just wanted …

sex?"

"That was a little cruel and a little crude, wasn't it?"

"Well, it is what it is …"

"Don't you judge me now …"

"I'm not."

I gulped down what was left of my sherry and placed my glass next to his. He was wearing a clean pair of jeans and a black T-shirt. Without considering my mother or Daniel for a second longer, I slid onto his lap and slowly, lifted his shirt. His dark curly hair was tied back, and his buckle was missing.

The higher I lifted his shirt, the more intrigued I became with that unbelievably powerful body. That cowboy was beautiful. Sensual. Strong. Macho. Perfect. His green eyes were starting to glisten, and his lips were slightly plumped up.

I unzipped his jeans and again, his tight-fitting Jockeys threatened to boycott me. Ryan reached down and lowered them to expose my brand-new obsession, leaving me slightly drunk and highly stirred. While admiring the physique that my body was threatening to fall in lust with, I could hardly wait for Ryan press me as close to him as he could.

When I kissed him again, his mouth tasted like spring and reminded me of a morning after a night of rainfall. I could feel him shifting below me, almost uncomfortably. I heard a faint grunt and moan, and when I looked into his eyes, he leaned back and rested his head on the coach with his eyes closed. Just like earlier in the river, Ryan's movements were in sync with mine and when I heard him moan out load, he grabbed onto me and pressed me down, leaving me unable to move.

I leaned forward and kissed him before I whispered in his ear, "There is nothing eight-seconds about you."

'Damn. I am getting so good at this.' It sounded so sexy, even to me.

He grabbed my head and pressed my mouth firmly onto his, kissing me fiercely while beginning to move frantically under me. I was ready to disappear from the moment. I could feel my body being transported back onto a summit I could only linger on for a short while. It had become my drug. An addiction I was ready and willing to admit and submit to.

I wanted to reach the top every chance I could. I wanted to stay there for longer and when I finally reached the peak, my entire being erupted into an explosive intensity.

He slid his arms around me and held me inflexibly against him. I trembled and quivered. My legs had grown weak, but I was not ready to come down just yet. I liked it there. I wanted to stay there. After a while, Ryan became still; he didn't move, so I clenched myself tighter around him.

I was slipping. Falling. The more I clasped at him, the closer I got back up to the summit. I had to get there again. I wanted to be there. I could feel him constrict around me once more, and when I squeezed my legs against his, the rush of tides, fluxes and waves began to set off millions of little trickles inside of me. I whimpered. I gasped. I breathed with difficulty. I just felt. I had victory and I savored my conquering the peak. I closed my eyes suddenly. I was there, on that summit and I never wanted to come down again.

I laid in his arms and waited patiently for my body to return to me. The shuddering was dwindling, and my breaths were returning to normal. Ryan wrapped his arms tighter around me and held me in silence. I retreated slightly, and stroked his flustered cheek,

"You, eight-second cowboy, are trouble."

He laughed from the very pit of his belly. His eyes were alive and for the first time, I noticed dimples on his cheeks. He was the alpha male, king of the jungle and the undisputed ruler of Ally Bradshaw's journey up to the summit. No doubts.

"And you Miss Bradshaw, might just steal my heart and take it home with you."

'Did he really have to say that? No. No. No.'

I quickly got up and pulled my jeans back on.

"Did I say something?"

After I was fully dressed, I turned to face him, flashing him my very best, fake smile, "No. I must go. My dad will probably wait up all night for me."

"See you tomorrow?"

"Sure."

I made a dash for it; a clean getaway and ran out through his front door, back into the fields that crossed over to the

Channing farm. It was cold; I was shivering and all I could think of was Daniel. If I am to be loved, I wanted it to be Daniel. I wanted Daniel against me. I wanted his skin against mine. I wanted his eyes on me, and I wanted his lips on my mouth. I wanted to lay on his chest and fall asleep again.

When I finally reached the farmhouse, I slowly walked up the stairs of the porch. It instantly struck me that Daniel was probably spending his evening with another woman. The date. Yay him! My stomach lurched at the thought, leaving me to almost choke on the vile building up inside of me. I could feel the blood drain from my face and knelt down slightly.

'Probably screwing her right at this very minute.'

That damn thought was driving me crazy and made me feel sick to my stomach. I slowly opened the front door and was instantly relieved that the house was quiet and dark. I peeked around the corner into the kitchen. It was dark. 'Oh, thank goodness.' I quietly made my way upstairs and stopped off at Max's bedroom again. When I peeked inside, I noticed both my parents asleep on his bed.

For a moment longer, I stood staring at them. My father had his arm protectively around her, while my mother's hand covered his. I missed them like that. I wished that they could be like that when the world wakes up in the morning.

It saddened me to realize how much destruction and devastation was left behind for us to deal with. My parents were struggling. Other than fighting to cope with Max's death, they were distraughtly clinging to what little was left of our family. My heart hurt for them. I was angry at my brother. His death destroyed my parents and the love my mother once had for me.

'Why did you have to get in that car, Max?'

The tears began seeping down my cheeks and when I walked into my bedroom, I collapsed onto my bed and cried. I cried for the brother I loved and lost. I wept for the mother who could barely stand the sight of me, and I sobbed for a father trying to hold it all together and change who he was, for me.

And as though that wasn't enough, I cried for Daniel. My heart ached for him. My soul hurt for him. I wanted to hear his voice. I wanted him to tell me that we're all going to be okay.

I slowly dialed his number. It was late, but I didn't care. My hands were trembling slightly and when I heard his familiar, soothing and comforting voice, my heart began to gallop wildly,

"Ally?"

"Are you asleep?"

"Sort of. I ... I can't really talk now ..."

I didn't know what to say. I knew that he wasn't alone. I didn't want to hear him tell me he couldn't talk. My heart missed a beat and my hands began to tremble. I knew without a doubt that Daniel was in the arms of someone else.

"Are you okay?" I could hear the sudden fear in his voice.

"I ... yes ... I am fine. I just wanted to check in."

My voice was throaty and husky. I did my best to hold my pose and hold back my tears.

"Ally, you don't sound fine? What's going on?"

"Nothing. I'm sorry I worried you … I shouldn't have called."

I ended the call at once and tossed my phone into a corner of my bedroom. I berated myself for feeling the way I felt. I hated feeling that way about Daniel, and I had no idea at all, how to explain the untaught emotions that were bringing me to, and keeping me on my knees.

My thoughts were instantly disrupted when my phone rang.

'Daniel.'

I walked over to the corner and picked it up. It was Daniel.

"Danny …"

"I'm coming to get you."

My heart broke out into a flutter when I heard the genuine fear, concern and determination in his voice. He cared.

"No, don't do that. I'm fine. My mom and I just had an argument. Nothing new. I just wanted to hear your voice."

"I can be there in a couple of hours."

"No, don't do that. I'll be back in a couple of days. I doubt I will be staying for more than a few more days. I'm fine, I promise. "Daniel didn't say another word, and after a few seconds of silence, he finally responded, "Alright. Promise you'll call if something's wrong."

"I promise. Enjoy your evening. Daniel … thank you …"

"Get some sleep, okay?"

"Okay." I smiled. He made my heart smile. He fixed my soul and fixed my heart. Daniel Sotherby, my fireman made my heart beam all over again.

I took a quick shower and climbed into bed. I laid staring at the ceiling and couldn't get the picture of my parents sleeping on Max's bed out of my mind. I was desperate for my mother to feel better. I wanted my dad to get his wife back. I wanted my mother back. I wanted Max to come home and fix the mess he left us with. I wanted him to peek in and hand us back our shattered hearts, glued back together. Not quite new again, but in one piece. Only Max could do that. I couldn't.

I wanted life to carry on even though Max wasn't coming back. I wanted to see my mother's beautiful smile again, and I wanted my dad to be able to dance with her in the kitchen again just like they used to when we were little, even if only one more time. I couldn't stand the greatest sadness that had filled and entirely consumed our home and our lives. It was as though I could cut the sorrow lingering in this house with a blunt knife. I was terrified. I was so scared that we would never recover from losing Max.

Alice VL

I DO (NOT) – AT THE RODEO

PART 4

"Ally … Ally …"

It was a soft, tender, rasping voice calling out to me. I didn't recognize the voice, but it sounded eerily calming as it continued to call out my name. It wasn't my mom, and it wasn't my dad. It wasn't a voice that I recognized as someone I knew, but I was quite sure I had heard it somewhere before.

I peered out over the covers and was instantly startled to find a man sitting at the end of my bed. As though a jolt rushed through me, I sat straight up and rubbed my sluggish eyes all at the same time. I shuddered when I was aware of a sudden, unexpected chill in the air.

I stared at him and tried to focus, instead I frowned. I simply couldn't take my eyes off the stranger sitting at the end of my bed, and even though I could not quite see past his silhouette, I remained eerily unruffled. I was not frightened or intimidated. I didn't feel any discomfort or fear for the uninvited man in my bedroom, in the darkest hours of the night. As my eyes adjusted to the image of the man in front of me, I was instantly aware of a slight shimmer, as though the air in front of him was warped and twisted. A pale, silvery light appeared behind him, making it easier for me to identify him. 'Am I dreaming? I must be dreaming.'

Alice VL

I DO (NOT) – AT THE RODEO

"Ally … it's me … Maxie …"

"Max?"

"Shhh …"

"Max, is it really you?"

I leaned forward and instantly flung my arms around him. It was my brother. My Max. I was dreaming; I knew I was dreaming, but I didn't care and I didn't want to wake up. I didn't want this dream to end. In all the years since Max's death, I had never once dreamed of him and while clinging to my brother, I realized that I had begun forgetting what he had looked like and more importantly, what he felt like.

"I've missed you so, so much Maxie …"

"I miss you guys too, Ally … well, not miss you all as much as I worry about you …"

His arms around me were strong and powerful. He hugged me tightly and held me close to him. I didn't want him to let go. I was terrified that I might forget how he felt, how he looked and how he smelled the moment I woke up.

"Ally … mom … you know?"

I recoiled slightly and frowned,

"I know Max. You've left her heart in a mess. She just can't function like she used to anymore, Maxie …"

"You have to help her, Ally. Mom is dying slowly … and she's taking dad with her."

Alice VL

I DO (NOT) – AT THE RODEO

"How? I don't know what to do? She doesn't listen to dad. She doesn't listen to me. Go look; go peek into your bedroom and see, they are both asleep on your bed. They will never get over this … you."

"I know Ally, I watch them and that's why I am here. You are here and you are the only one that can help them. I have been waiting so long for you to come home again and now that you're here, together, you and I can bring them back. You have to listen carefully to me Ally; I know you think this is nothing more than a dream that you'll forget in the morning, but just humor me. In my closet, at the bottom in a corner is a chest with birthday cards from grandma that I have kept since I was a little boy. In there is a letter I wrote mom when I was little. I was really sick, and I thought I was going to die."

"Really?"

"Remember when I had that virus none of the doctors could diagnose? I must have been twelve or thirteen?"

"Yeah?"

"I wrote mommy a letter. I was so scared that I would die without telling her the things I should have told her when I was alive. I want you to get that letter and give it to her. I want to tell her those things now."

"Max, you're making me sad. Dreams aren't supposed to be this sad."

"Just promise me you will do that for me? Give her that letter and tell her about your dream. Tell her about tonight. Tell her that I am happy, but that they're make it hard for me to let go. Tell them it's later than they think. Try and remember everything about you and me here, Ally."

"Maxie … I will try, but mommy doesn't listen to me."

"Dad blames himself, sissy. I don't know why, but he does. Mom blames him too and it's just not right. You need to tell dad that I took my eyes off the road for only a second. I was speeding even after he scolded me a thousand times before; I was speeding. When my car left the road, I clearly heard dad warning me again to mind my speed and recklessness. Never to speed. It was never his fault, Ally. I didn't listen to him and I should have. It was just an accident, nothing more, okay? Do you hear me?"

I felt my tears escape from the corners of my eyes while a confining lump in my throat began throbbing stronger than ever before.

"And you, Ally. Be happy. Do more of what makes you happy. I'm glad you kicked that son of a bitch to the curb."

I burst out laughing as the tears continued to gush from my eyes.

"You have to help mama, Ally. Please, let me rest."

"She hates me, Max."

"No, she doesn't. She's scared of getting hurt again. Mom didn't change after I left. Sure, she was sad, and she grieved for me, but she really changed when you married Michael and left. You have to find a way to get back to her, Ally."

Alice VL

I DO (NOT) – AT THE RODEO

"I love you so much, Maxie … you left us all in such a mess."

"I love you too, sissy and I know I messed up and for that, I am sorry. Just know that I am here always, and I would never exchange my new home for that one again. And just so you know … that fireman, someday, you'll see that he's the best thing that's ever happened to you."

Alice VL

"Ally!"

I opened my eyes again. I anxiously glanced around me, but there was no-one. Max was gone. I was instantly annoyed that my mother had woken me, and tore me away from Max. I frantically searched my bedroom and looked around me for any evidence that would suggest that Max was there. I looked down at the edge of my bed, hoping for an indentation, a crinkle in my throw or a hair that might have fallen out of Max's head, but there was nothing. There was not a single thing that would point to Max being there and after letting out an enormous sigh, I accepted the fact that he was never there. It was nothing more than a lousy dream. My heart hurt. My gut hurt. My soul was sore.

"Ally!"

My mother's voice echoed throughout the house, leaving me angry and completely despondent. I slid grumpily out of bed just as she appeared in my doorway,

"Are you up?"

"Almost."

"Well hurry up. Pastor Carmichael is on his way over."

'Oh Lord, mother.'

"Oh mother. Really?"

"Hurry up. He'll be here in thirty minutes."

'This is all I need right now. And that right there is why I never come home.'

I slipped on a pair of cotton pants with a matching tank top. Once I had tied the laces on my Tomy's, I quickly made my way to the staircase. Reflecting back on my dream, I stopped and stared straight ahead of me. Max was adamant and convincing when he instructed me where to find the chest and told what to do with a supposed letter inside. It was all so vivid and clear, and I couldn't help but wonder whether the letter he claimed to be in his closet, really was there?

'It was just a dream Ally.'

Dream, reality or not, I wanted to check. I quickly glanced around me, and was extra cautious that no-one saw me slip into Max's bedroom. I could hear my parents' voices coming from the kitchen when I softly closed his bedroom door behind me. I walked up to his closet and nervously opened his cupboard doors.

It all was exactly as it was before Max died. Not a thing was moved; not a shirt was out of place or a pair of shoes touched. For sixteen years, my mother refused to even go as far as to re-organize his closet. I bent down and searched frantically for the chest that was supposedly in a corner somewhere. I couldn't see it, but as I was about to give up, I felt what I thought to be a wooden box. When I pulled it closer, I smiled and recognized Max's handwriting,

'Max's stuff.'

My heart had broken out into a gallop and with trembling hands, I lifted the lid, and just as he said in my dream, all

I DO (NOT) – AT THE RODEO

Grandma Joan's birthday cards were neatly tied together. I carefully lifted the pile of cards, and right at the bottom was a white, folded sheet of paper. The tears began to blind me slightly when I took the handwritten letter out, before I placed the cards back into the box.

I opened the letter. I couldn't believe that it was there. I couldn't quite wrap my head around the fact that exactly what Max had told me in my dream, was in that little wooden chest, just as he said it would be. After all the years and especially, after all the tears, there was finally something from Max. My hands were cold and were quivering violently. My legs suddenly gave way under me, forcing me to sit down on the carpet before I opened his letter.

The tears begin to bucket relentlessly from my eyes as my heart continued to skip beat after beat. 'What if it wasn't a dream? What if Max was here?'

'Dear Mama,

If you get this letter, it'll mean that I am gone and it will mean that you are sad. But mama, I won't be gone. You see, I've been talking to my angel and he said that all it is, is just me slipping out. Like just into another room. You can't see me, but I can see you.

Mama, I love you and I am so scared that you will be sad forever. I don't want you to cry for me. I am going to be with Jesus; I know I am, He said so. I am going to live in Heaven and I'll wait for you, dad and Ally to come home.

But mommy, if you're going to be sad that I am with

Jesus, then I'm not going to be able to keep an eye on you because it will make me too sad. And I really want to slip in now and again because I am going to miss you too.

Please tell daddy and Ally I love them and please ask them not to cry for me. Tell daddy that I wish I could grow up and work on the farm with him.

Mommy, look after my sissy. Tell her I love her even if we fight. Please don't let her be sad.

I love you mommy. Forever.

From Jesus' lap,

Your son, Maxwell Channing.'

'This is so typical of the twelve-year-old Max I can remember.'

The tears were streaming irrepressibly down my face. I trembled fiercely and sobbed for the brother I missed so terribly. 'What Max must have gone through then? How did we never know this? How did we never find this letter?'

I laid down on the carpet in front of his closet when everything inside me began to hurt. My eyes were blurry and the sounds around me seemed incredibly far away.

I pulled my knees up to my chin and began rocking back and forth. I missed my brother. I wished with all my heart I could trade places with him. I wished I could bring him back to my mother but more than anything, I wished he never climbed into that damn Mustang. I wished he could come back.

I DO (NOT) – AT THE RODEO

"Ally?"

My mother knelt behind me and gently wiped the tears from my cheeks.

"Ally?"

I sat upright and took her hand into mine. She sat down beside me and nervously squeezed my hand.

"I miss him too, Ally."

"I know, mama."

I frantically swabbed at the tears, desperate to compose myself before I handed her Max's letter.

"Mama … he was here … last night …"

"Who, Max? What are you talking about, Ally?"

"Max … he was here …"

"Oh Ally … you just had a bad dream. Come here …"

She wrapped her arms around me and held me tightly against her. 'Roses. I smell roses. And love.'

"I sometimes forget that you and your father are going through this too …"

She rested her head on my shoulder and pressed me snugger to her. "Mama … you have to listen to me. I don't want you to say anything until I'm finished."

She sat upright and took my hand again.

Alice VL

"He told me that … there are cards in his closet that he kept that Grandma sent each year for his birthday. He said that, when he was sick that time when he had the virus … he said he thought he was going to die so he wrote you a letter."

The frown on my mother's face was inimitable. I prayed desperately that Max's letter to her would finally bring her closure.

"I checked mama. It was there, just like he said."

I handed the letter over to her and when she reached for it, her hands were vibrating slightly. She opened the letter and as she began to read Max's last letter to her, the tears had started to gush from her eyes. With each drop that landed on the letter, the ink smudged and almost drowned out his words.

"Oh God, Ally."

"I know, mommy."

I placed my arms around her and held her protectively against me. 'Roses.'

"He wants me to tell dad that it was just an accident. He looked down for just a second. He was speeding, and he could hear daddy warning him. He said that he could hear dad telling him that it was never okay to speed … and that he hates it that dad blames himself."

I looked around and noticed my dad standing in the doorway, the tears streaming from his eyes,

"It wasn't your fault daddy. It was nobody's fault. It was

Alice VL

just an accident and Max is sorry. He doesn't want to see you like this because he is here. He is always here; with us and around us. He sees everything."

My dad walked up to us and placed an arm around both my mother and I. I rested my head on his chest as he pulled my mother closer to him.

"Jason, this has to stop. We have a daughter who is very much alive. What are we doing? Max is gone. We must let him rest. We are not letting him rest."

My dad sobbed viciously. I wept sadistically, and my mother was doing her best to hold it all together. My father got up and quickly made his way to the door before he turned around,

"Max loves you daddy, and he knows you guys, we … all love him, but he wants you to know … none of this was ever your fault."

He wiped the tears from his cheeks before he walked out. I heard him hurriedly make his way downstairs and I couldn't help but hear him let out a dejected sigh. My father was crushed.

I turned back to my mother who had neatly folded Max's letter,

"Mama … I will never leave you. I will always come home to you. You will never lose me. You are my home, mommy …"

"I know baby … I was just so scared of losing both my children that I ended up pushing you away anyway. I just can't go through this again."

I DO (NOT) – AT THE RODEO

My heart hurt for her. I didn't understand how she could ever could have thought I would leave her. I placed my arms around her and held her against me. I love her.

"I'm not going anywhere, mama. I will always come home."

I wiped the warm tears from her cheeks and for the first time since Max died, I saw a slight, but loving, unforced smile on her face.

"Are you happy, Ally?"

"Yes mama. I am now. I truly am."

"You know, Michael never really deserved you …"

"Thank you, mommy. Thank you for saying that. I like my life exactly as it is now. I like that I can go home alone and dance to my own tune."

"You know, and if you ever tell your father … I'll deny it, but I was a little tramp when I was a teenager …"

"Mom!"

"Shhh … they were the best years of my life. How do you think I knew it was your dad I wanted to spend the rest of my life with? I had to test the rest before I settled on the best."

'Oh. My. Word!' We both burst out laughing and slowly, the tears began to dry on both our cheeks. It felt good. It felt as though a mountain had been lifted off my shoulders and my mom felt like home again. 'Thank you, Maxie.'

Alice VL

I DO (NOT) – AT THE RODEO

We spent the next ten minutes laughing and chattering, something we hadn't done in years. I told my mom about Michael and how disgusted I was by him. I told her about Daniel and how he sometimes invades my mind. I told her about William Walker and how cold and isolated I felt around him.

And then, I told her about Ryan Henderson, Water Hill's eight-second cowboy and how swept off my feet I was. My mother listened closely and hung on every word I was saying. She laughed often, but more importantly, she laughed loudly and from her belly.

"Ally, I wish I was a fly on your wall when Lily walked in and found Michael all stripped and ready for action!"

"I know, right? That's exactly what I said!"

Sigh

"Not that it would really have been much fun given the story he came up with."

"I can't believe I thought you could actually drug him?"

I burst out laughing and placed my arms around my mother's neck. 'Roses.'

"Now that I think of it, it could probably be something I would do, mama. I'm still learning."

She smiled and gently stroked my cheek, but when we heard the doorbell ring, my mom stared at me and began to panic. "Shit. It's Reverend Carmichael."

I DO (NOT) – AT THE RODEO

"You said shit."

My mother giggled and quickly got up to leave, "Come on … help me get rid of the man."

I jumped up and quickly followed my mother downstairs. When we reached the living room, my dad had invited him in and was sitting across from him in the living room.

Reverend Carmichael rose to his feet and kissed my mother on the cheek before he turned to me and offered me an extended hand. I shook his hand and smiled as innocently as I could,

"I've heard so much about you, Ally."

'Oh boy. I can just imagine.'

"Reverend … today is not a good day. My daughter and I made plans and it completely slipped my mind."

My dad frowned, grinned and shook his head.

"Oh alright. It sounded urgent when you called?"

He leaned closer to my mother and whispered softly,

"Didn't you say something about her drugging her husband?"

"I don't think so? You must have misunderstood. He claims she drugged him, but it turns out, he's the real asshole."

I gulped. My father huffed, and Reverend Carmichael gasped for air. I couldn't help but snigger loudly at my mother's ability to use the word 'asshole', but at that very moment, I was enormously proud of my mother.

"But, she divorced him. She committed an act of adultery."

"No, Reverend. The only adulterer here is Michael Bradshaw and Ally did well to kick his lying, cheating and pathetic ass to the curb."

'She said ass!' Reverend Carmichael's eyes grew bigger. I don't think he has ever heard my mother speak like that.

"Mrs. Channing. It would serve you well if you changed your attitude and minded your language. It's not hard to see where Ally gets her mannerisms from."

"Revvie …"

'Revvie! Oh Lord. Revvie?' It seems that I was not the only one with vocabulary issues in the Channing house.

My mother placed an arm around him and led him out to the front door. My dad and I could do nothing more than stare at my mother, stunned by her sudden untaught behavior.

"My little girl is not going to start dying while she's alive, do you understand? And between you and me, if she wants to screw every single man out there, and it makes her happy … it makes me happy. Get it? Now, that does not make her a bad person. It merely makes her a sinner, but that's why we have you, isn't it so Revvie? Church is for sinners, not for saints. Not so?"

Reverend Carmichael gasped for air once again. My dad

and I were intrigued and followed them out to the entrance hall. I burst out laughing when my mother calmly informed him that 'Revvie' was there to forgive my sins. Hilarious!

"I have nothing more to say, Mrs. Channing. I will pray for you and I will pray for Ally tonight."

"Good. We are counting on that. Now goodbye, and please stop by later for pie and cake at the fair."

When the door closed behind him, my father and I were overcome with shock and were instantly silenced. My mother turned and peered over at us before she burst out laughing while the tears were streaming down her face.

"Did you see his face?"

My mother whispered through the laughter that quickly turned into an uproarious hilarity with tears continuing to gush from her eyes. My dad and I followed, and broke out into a fit of hysterics before my dad placed his arms around us and drew us closer to him,

"Oh Lord. The South has risen again."

Alice VL

I DO (NOT) – AT THE RODEO

Alice VL

PART 5

After breakfast, my parents and I loaded their truck and drove out to the fair. We were all smiles and I couldn't help but savor each moment with them. I was glad I was home. There were a couple of times I was sure I saw my mom grab my dad's bum when she thought that no-one was looking.

Each time, my dad's face would stifle, and my mom would titter. It was wonderful seeing them like that again. I couldn't quite place my finger on the last time I saw my mother show my father any sort of affection.

Once the tables were set up, and the cakes and pies were displayed; once my dad began taking the children for their rides, I quickly excused myself and set out to find Ryan.

I couldn't help but think of Daniel and each time the idea that he was seeing someone came to mind, it felt to me as though I was losing my mind.

But, I was in Water Hills and I had Ryan to distract me. Somehow, and without him knowing it, he consoled me. Ryan took me away from all my realities and lifted me higher and higher than Daniel or William ever did. He pulled me out of a hole I began to sink into, and hurled me into a place I had never been in before.

Alice VL

Still, it didn't change or substitute the emotions brewing inside of me, and it didn't lessen my intense need and dire craving for Daniel.

"Ryan!"

I caught a glimpse of him stacking bales of hay in the stables.

"Hello beautiful. You're smiling?"

"Yep. I had a sort of great morning with my mom."

"That's great!"

"You busy?" I didn't want to stick around for too long and had a sudden urge to go back to the kiosk.

"Just finished. But the rodeo is about to start?"

"I can't stay. I want to help my mom out today. Can we meet up tonight?"

"My place?"

"How about the river?"

"Alright. I'll meet you there at eight?"

"Perfect. See you later."

On my way back to my mom's stall, I heard Heather call out behind me,

"Ally!"

I DO (NOT) – AT THE RODEO

I stopped and for a moment, I stood unresponsively before I turned around. 'What does she want?' At once, I was reminded of my dream, or visit, or whatever you want to call it with Max the night before.

He loved Heather. It was never her fault that Max died. Still, I couldn't quite get past the fact that she was moving on without him. It would be what Max would have wanted; I knew that, I just wished he would have told me that the night before.

If I were to ask Max, I was pretty sure that he would have told me that his biggest wish was for Heather to find someone who loved her, and to have the family she had always wanted.

It's just, I didn't. I didn't want her to move on. I didn't want her to forget Max. I didn't ever want her to find better than Max. I wanted her to mourn him and miss him just as we do.

'Be nice, Ally.'

"Heather …"

She looked odd running up to me with that enormous belly of hers. I couldn't help but snigger unashamedly at the sight and when she finally reached me, she was gasping for breath.

"Pfew. Let me just catch my breath."

I chuckled again. What Max ever saw in her, I will never understand.

"So, I saw you out at the barn with Ryan the other night."

'Oh Lord. Really?'

Alice VL

"You did? We were probably just …"

"Just … yeah right. What would your parents say if they caught you hanky-pankying with that cowboy in the barn?

Pankying? Is that even a word? *sigh* Did she see us?

"Were you spying on me? And how is it any of your business who I am hanky-pankying with?"

"No. I was looking for Ryan when I saw you two … uhm … together like that."

I lowered my head in shame. The idea of Heather seeing Ryan and I together like that was horrifying.

"Don't worry, I won't tell your parents, but you must stop it. My friend Georgia has been out with him a few times, and I'd hate for Ryan to break her heart. She really likes him and he likes her too."

'Georgia?'

"He's dating?"

"Yes. Sort of."

"What does sort-of mean? Oh, never mind, I don't want to know. I'll see what I can do."

"Good. I'm glad we understand each other."

In a huff, she turned around and as though she was mimicking a duck, she stormed off and made her way back to the rodeo rink. I did nothing more, but shake my head. 'What did she see?' I could only hope that it wasn't as explicit as I knew it was. Not wanting to give it another thought, I turned around and made my way back to my mother's stall.

"Ally? I thought you were at the rodeo?"

I settled into a seat next to my mom and smiled. 'I like this.'

"I wanted to spend the day with you …"

She beamed from ear to ear. Right there, I decided that Sylvia Channing was the most beautiful woman in the world.

"If you don't mind, mama … I'd like to take Morgan out tonight?"

Morgan is my mom's prized horse. My grandfather gifted him to her a month before he unexpectedly passed away. She was enormously protective of him and never allowed him at the fair. He is hers and for her alone to ride.

"Sure … would you like papa to go with you?"

"No, I'm meeting Ryan at the river."

"Oh my … he is a rather handsome devil."

We both burst out laughing and when my father appeared almost out of nowhere, we shot blank stares at each other and giggled.

"What's so funny girls?"

"Nothing dad …"

I DO (NOT) – AT THE RODEO

"I was just telling Ally what a handsome devil you are …"

"Oh, mama bear … stop teasing."

My dad turned bright red at once and I suddenly realized where I got it from. We all burst out laughing. I had never before seen my dad as bashful as at that very moment.

'It's good to be home.'

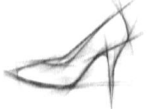

Alice VL

I DO (NOT) – AT THE RODEO

At just before eight that evening, I ran downstairs and found my mother seated at the kitchen table, drinking her last cup of tea for the evening.

"I'm on my way, mom. Is there anything I can do before I go?"

She at once got up from her chair and handed me a picnic basket.

"No. I'm going to turn in early. I hope your father joins me … wink-wink. I've packed you some eats and a nice bottle of wine."

'Wait. Hang on. Is she planning on hanky-pankying with my dad tonight? Oh, my hat.' There was that word pankying again. I rather liked that word.

"Thank you, mama."

"You're welcome, my lovey."

'My lovey.' I couldn't remember when last my mother called me my 'lovey.' I took the basket and turned to walk away before it suddenly hit me right between the eyes; when last have I told my mom that I loved her?

"Mom?"

"Yes, my girl?"

"I love you, and I'm glad to be home."

She glowered, smiled and slowly walked up to me before she placed a hand on my cheek, "I am sorry, Ally. For everything.

Alice VL

I DO (NOT) – AT THE RODEO

I've made so many mistakes with you, but please know, I have never not loved you. I love you."

My heart smiled. My soul was happy. I turned around suddenly and quickly made my way through the front door and onto the porch. I did my best to hide the tears, only this time, they were happy tears.

"Dad? You scared me!"

He was sitting on the porch in the dark, just like he always did. Every night. Without fail. He placed his cigarette down and stood up from his chair,

"You behave tonight, okay?"

I sniggered softly. 'No chance of that.'

"I will, daddy. Why don't you and mom do something tonight?"

"Do something like what?"

"I don't know dad. Put some music on and dance with her."

"Your mother will think I have totally lost the plot."

"No, she won't. She misses you daddy. Remember how you two used to dance in the kitchen? Do that."

He smiled sadly and placed his arms around me before he hugged me tightly. It was one of those bear hugs I had missed so much.

Alice VL

I DO (NOT) – AT THE RODEO

"Go on … she's waiting for you …"

When my dad closed the front door behind him, I smiled again. I stood staring at the closed door for what felt like forever, before I hastily made my way over to the barn. When I spotted Morgan, I was pleasantly surprised to find him all saddled up and rearing to go.

'Must have been dad.'

I fastened the picnic basket onto him and climbed on.' I've missed this.' We walked slowly out of the stable and trotted into the fields, and down the path that led to the river. From a distance, I could see a flickering light coming from what I presumed to be a paraffin lamp.

'He's already there.'

When Morgan and I reached him, he got up from the blanket he was sitting on, and immediately walked over to us.

"I thought you stood me up?"

I gazed intently at him. He had never looked as good as he looked that night. I was not sure what it was, and decided that perhaps the stars that were shining so brightly around a moon that was fully out, was responsible for the way he looked.

Was it because the reflection of the stars on the water were so mesmerizing? Was it because he looked so devilish handsome in a brand-new pair of jeans, white T-shirt and that damn buckle? I couldn't quite decide. Was it perhaps because being back home was nothing like I thought it would be?

Alice VL

"Never."

I slowly climbed off Morgan and unstrapped the picnic basket.

"Great minds think alike."

Ryan suddenly pointed out to another picnic basket on the blanket.

"My mother …"

I chuckled bashfully and touched his arm,

"You're kidding! This was my mother too!"

We both burst out laughing before he tied Morgan to a tree. I walked over to the quilted blanket that was neatly spread out on the ground and sat down smiling. Ryan sat down beside me and we both stared out over the river.

"So … Georgia?"

His eyes widened, but he shook his head and faced downwards.

"What have you heard?"

I snickered softly. It was not my intention to embarrass him, "Heather cornered me today and warned me to stay away from you. You are 'sort of' dating Georgia."

He shook his head again.

"I mean, she's a lovely girl and I probably would have if

you didn't come along."

'Oh no.' I didn't know what to say.

"Ryan … I'm going to be going back in a couple of weeks. If you like her, you should date her."

I didn't want to flat out tell him that I was not at all interested in a serious relationship, or that I had no plans to come back to live in Water Hills. 'There was still Daniel.'

"But … I like you too …"

He whispered and gazed unswervingly at me. I liked Ryan. A lot. I was obsessed with his body and I was drawn to his smell. But, it was just that. Nothing more.

"You should date her."

"You don't see anything happening between us, Ally?"

Why can't a girl just have good old-fashioned sex without feelings getting in the way?

"No, I don't. I mean, not really. Surely you don't either?"

"The idea did cross my mind …"

"Ryan … I was married for twelve awful years. I like this. I'm not leaving Willow County. My life is there, and yours is here … you should totally date Georgia."

"I guess … I just really, really like you."

He suddenly looked unbearably sad. I felt awful. Horrible.

Alice VL

I DO (NOT) – AT THE RODEO

I lifted myself off the blanket and onto his lap. Clasping his face into my hands, I gazed deeply into those murky, puddled green eyes. 'Gosh, what a beautiful man.'

"We've got tonight. Tomorrow, is tomorrow, okay? I really, really like you too but I am not ready for committing to anything more than one day at a time."

I kissed him tenderly. He placed his arms around me and pulled me closer to him, before he began kissing me with increased desire and yearning. My stomach turned, and my breaths grew shorter once again. I could feel Ryan grasp at me with immense strength, and I was instantly irritated by the fact that I had worn jeans.

'Shit.'

With two anxious hands, I unzipped his jeans, while I grew increasingly obsessed with the way he felt. I had no desire for a long, drawn-out session. I was penetratingly attracted to him and could think of nothing else than feeling him against me.

Ryan unzipped my jeans and when I lifted myself up, he pulled them off me with almost no effort at all. He seemed extremely well-trained and definitely well-equipped at getting my jeans off me in almost no time at all. I couldn't help but wonder how many times he had done that before. I didn't care. I was once again amazed by his strength and how smoothly he could undress me.

I climbed back onto him and pressed my body against his. He held me tightly against him and lifted his head just enough to meet my eyes. He gazed intently at me, making me slightly uncomfortable. I lowered my head and kissed him, desperate to get his eyes off mine. His lips were slightly distended, and his cheeks were somewhat flustered. He moved slowly, and I happily joined in, and adjusted to his rhythm.

It was only a moment later that he clutched firmly at my hips and held me down before he stopped moving. I could feel him pulsate and I could feel the ever-familiar triggers inside of me going off one by one, until a blast went off unexpectedly but right on schedule.

Ryan was not moving, and when he buried his head in my chest, I could feel a shudder rip through his entire body. His grunting was soft and slow. I was out of breath and waited patiently for my body that had not quite begun to recover from the intense quaking that wholly engulfed me, to return to normal.

I looked at him and smiled. 'Georgia is a damn lucky girl.' When Ryan's body finally began to relax, I slowly climbed off him and slid on my jeans. He hurriedly zipped up his jeans, and poured us each a glass of wine.

"I'd prefer it if you'd buy me a drink first."

I chuckled shyly,

"I told you, you're trouble cowboy."

The next few days were almost magical. I spent the remaining of my days of the festival between my parents and the rodeo. Despite my initial reservations of returning home to Water Hills, it turned out to be just what I needed. I enjoyed my parents' company again and was once again reminded of the carefree, untroubled life that awaited me at home.

It was an enormous relief to witness my parents change slowly in the days that followed my dream of Max. It was as if his letter was all they needed to get back to basics, deal with their sorrow, and truly live again.

My mother and I spent our evenings getting to know each other again. I was pleasantly surprised to discover things about her that I never knew before. It was like visiting with an old friend again as we slowly began packing up Max's belongings shortly after my mom made the decision to move forward, and turn his bedroom into a study, or as we call it, a man-cave for my dad.

My father seemed lighter, younger and far happier than I could remember. There was a spring in his step; one I had never seen before, even as a child. As was habitual, he would sit out on the porch in the evenings, but the moment my mom would peer her head around the corner and excuse herself, my dad would follow shortly. In the days that followed, I could ignore the permanent smile on his face, and I could only guess that my mom had something to do with it.

I decided to slip out at night and meet up with Ryan either at the stalls, the barn or at the river. I wanted to be careful; I didn't want to spoil the relationship I was starting to recover with my parents. I had no intention of shaming them, especially after my mother's harsh encounter with 'Revvie.'

I wanted to behave. For them. But, the more time I spent with Ryan, the more I liked him. I had fallen in lust with him, just as I once did with Daniel.

Yet, even though I still felt a connection with Daniel, I had learned, and I have realized that sex would differ with each man, and that I was not yet ready to commit myself to only one. There was still far too much to discover, and way too little time left.

Daniel hadn't texted or called me again. That left me feeling insecure and somewhat disappointed. It left me feeling anxious and convinced that his patience had run out with me. I was overcome with paranoia and the thoughts of him actually dating someone, almost drove me. The idea of wine, roses and a relationship with another woman was killing me slowly. 'Yes, I know. I asked for this.'

Whatever it was, I found myself day-dreaming of him at the worst of times. I hated that he had such a powerful hold over me. I wished I knew, and could understand exactly what it was I was feeling, but I continually tried to convince myself that it was nothing more than an obsession with the first man that gave me my very first ticket into a world of magic. It had to be. Period. 'That's what I'll keep telling myself.'

On the last night of the Annual Fall Festival, a last barn dance was scheduled to end off our fabulous week of rodeos, horse riding, stalls and festivities.

There would be an enormous, some call it an earth-shattering fireworks display, a barbeque and loads of fun and games. Afterwards, while the younger of us were at the barn dance, the older folks would settle onto the lawn and watch a classic, old-fashioned black and white Charlie Chaplin movie, as was tradition each year.

I DO (NOT) – AT THE RODEO

I was excited to attend the last barn dance of the year and I was secretly happy to spend it with Ryan. I chose a flowing, short'ish skirt with a tank top and a denim jacket that I rounded off with proper country boots and Max's cowboy hat. I didn't feel sexy, I felt pretty. I felt as though I blended in and sort of, belonged in Water Hills again.

The fireworks display was magnificent and lit up the entire town of Water Hills. Ryan and I were both stunned by the enchantment around us, but each time I peered over at Heather, she shot invisible blades at me. She absolutely unsettled me.

When the display was over, the youngsters hurriedly huddled into the barn while the rest, including my parents, laid their blankets down on the lawn in front of an enormous screen that was brought out earlier.

I was not in the mood for Heather's judgmental glares and quickly turned to Ryan, "Let's go to the stables ..."

He smiled and winked in approval, and when I noticed the sheer delight on his face, he took my hand into his,

"I thought you'd never ask!"

With my hand firmly clutched in his, I followed him while secretly looking around me and hoping that nobody would see us. I would hate for anyone to catch a glimpse of us slipping into the stables, while everyone else was either in the barn or on the lawn.

When we reached the stables, I quickly turned around. I glanced around me one more time and was relieved that no-one was in sight.

I closed the stable door and ran up to Ryan. I smiled and stood quietly in front of him. I was slightly nervous. He had already taken off his shirt and stared back at me for a moment longer. For just a second, I wanted to stop and admire the perfect cowboy standing in front of me.

I walked closer to him and placed my arms around him. My ruby red, faded hair was loose and flowing down my back. I felt pretty. Girly. I felt special.

He bent down and kissed me before he placed his hands on my hips and pressed me firmly against him. I could feel his passion for me grow, and was at once, entirely swept off my feet.

Again. I was in love. The only problem with that was, it was not with a man, but with the adrenalin that pumped through my veins each time I was swept away and placed on Ryan Henderson's summit.

I was in love with feeling another body against mine. I was in love with a body that was forbidden and hidden from me, and from the world. I was besotted with the way he made me feel, and I was infatuated with the idea that he wouldn't be the last.

He picked me, and that made me feel wanted. With all those thoughts rushing around inside of me, I quickly freed him from those damn challenging Jockeys with instant success. He lifted me up against him, before I folded my legs around him. At once, I begin to quiver shamelessly.

I moaned softly and realized that my eight-second

cowboy was responsible for sounds I just couldn't seem to, or even care to muffle. He pushed me into the stable wall and drove ruthlessly into me. When my whimpering grew louder, he pressed his lips against mine, desperate to silence me.

"Ally?"

'Wait. Hang on. I know that voice. And it's not Ryan's. Shit.'

I stopped moving and didn't want to turn around. I was horrified. I was in a compromising position, in the arms of a cowboy, in the stables with my parents only a few feet from me.

Ryan didn't move either and stared at me. After standing there motionlessly for just a moment longer, I finally turned around and gazed over in the direction of the stable door only to discover my father standing there. I was horrified. 'This cannot be happening,'

'Oh Lord. This cannot be happening.' Ryan and I were both stunned, silenced and instantly ashamed. My father turned around at once, and without saying a word, he quickly walked off.

When Ryan placed me back down on the ground, he swiftly pulled up his jeans. We didn't say a word to one other. I was mortified, and Ryan turned ashen and I could instantly hear familiar sounds coming from what was supposed to be the movie.

I stared in astonishment at Ryan, "Charlie Chaplin is a silent movie, isn't it?"

I frowned and tried to decipher where the voices were

coming from. That in no way at all, even sounded like an ordinary movie. Still dazed and awkward, Ryan and I walked out and from the other side of the stable door, we had a perfect view of the big screen.

It was Ryan and I in full view of an audience of about a hundred people. It was a live recording of us in the stables, and it was being played repeatedly.

I was humiliated. I wanted to die. Once again, all I wanted was for the ground to open up beneath my feet and swallow me whole. I could only imagine what my parents must have thought of me. 'No wonder my dad stormed into the stables …'

Slowly and anxiously, I made my way to where my parents were. I knew without a fraction of doubt that it was Heather's doing. I was livid. Enraged. Disgusted, and totally humiliated.

Ryan, who hadn't said a word at all, followed slowly behind me, unsure of what to do next. I felt terrible for him, and hoped that it all would blow over soon.

When I reached the crowd on the lawn, I noticed my dad walk up to the screen. He turned around to face the audience, and for a moment, he stood in silence. I wanted to cry. We had just started building on our tainted and broken relationship. He had never been happier than the last few days, now this.

"Can you please stop this?"

He was looking in the direction of the projector. I let out an enormous sigh and felt horrible for putting my parents in such a degrading position.

I never wanted to humiliate them like that, especially at the point they had finally reached in their lives. For the first time in my life, my relationship with my parents was on track, only to be spoiled by the fact that I couldn't behave myself, even for only a few short days. It was awful watching my father standing there.

I was mortified, frozen to the spot. I stood silently, absorbing the cruelty of it all; the whispers and giggles that were making my head spin. I knew at that very moment that the folks of Water Hills would never forget what they had seen on the screen only minutes before. It was destined become the topic of conversation for years to come, leaving my parents red-faced and traumatized.

When the film was finally stopped, my dad didn't move a finger. He stood staring at my mother before he glanced out over the townsfolk. He gazed over at me before he turned his attention back to the audience.

"Whoever is responsible for this, is disgraceful. To the person that thought they could embarrass my daughter, here's a little message for you. Ally Bradshaw is my child, and I am proud of her. If you were hoping to humiliate her, or us, you would have to do a lot better than this. Ally is a beautiful, young and single woman who is exploring her sexuality. She has committed no crime here, but the person who infringed on her privacy and made this video should be utterly ashamed. Now that's a crime and one I am going to make you pay for. Ally is a good girl, and always has been. She has a beautiful heart and an amazing spirit, and if she fancies a cowboy who is single and available, then who are we to judge her? You should be ashamed of yourself. My daughter carries no shame, and nor do her mother or I. We will never speak of this again, and if I ever find out who was responsible for this, rest assured that the mighty hand of the law will rain down on you and you will wish that you were never born."

I was shocked. Stunned. Lost for words. Disoriented. In my wildest dreams, I never could have anticipated my father coming forward, speaking on my behalf and standing up for me in my defense. Never did I think it was possible for my father to go against his community, one he had helped build, and defend my actions. My wild, unladylike actions. He had every reason to be angry and disgusted by my behavior. Instead, he unconditionally stood behind me, and loved me no matter what.

He had every right to be angry. Disappointed. He had the right to reprimand me and banish me from his home and his life forever. Instead, he chose to love, accept and support me. Jason Channing was my hero.

I glanced over to where my mom was sitting. I was anxious. I had never intended to disappoint her, but more than anything in the world, I never wanted her to be ashamed of me. She stood up slowly and walked over to where my father was standing. When she reached him, she kissed him lovingly before she turned to face the audience,

"Let one man here tell my they don't sin, then he can cast the first stone. You Mrs. Baker, does your husband know of your late-night escapades with Josiah Harper behind the old mill? And you, Mr. Sheldon, how many bottles of gin are buried in your garden? Do you think we don't know why your garden is so lovely and why you spend your days gardening on your belly? Then there's Mr. Shephard. We all know that his wife Dolly does not accidentally walk into doors and fall down stairs when we see a new bruise or a fresh black eye. Oh, and let's not forget Mrs. Carlson who quietly took thousands from her job at the school, and who has subsequently agreed to pay back the money hush hush. What about the Wilsons' who spend way too much time over at the Sanderson's and vice-versa? A swinger's lifestyle can be a bummer when the wrong lady leaves the wrong house in the mornings. And finally, Mrs. Collins who teaches the twelfth grade; is screwing teenage boys part of your curriculum?"

Everyone gasped and glanced frantically around them. You could hear a pin drop as she socked it to the holier than thou residents of Water Hills. I was shocked. Proud. Speechless. I was absolutely flabbergasted. I giggled nervously while the entire Water Hills community one by one got up, and quietly slipped out of the fair.

In a million years, I could never have imagined my mother come forward and damn the entire population of Water Hills to hell. She did it with a certain grace and elegance I had forgotten she was capable of, and in a way that they actually looked forward to their trip.

This was the mother I remembered. This was the woman I once admired. The fighter. The wolf who came in like a wrecking ball. That woman standing there addressing the crowd, was my mother. I was home, and my roots were firmly planted in Water Hills, with them.

Alice VL

I DO (NOT) – AT THE RODEO

For this first time in my life, I looked at mother and saw her in a whole new light. I admired her and enormously respected her. I was bemused. I was gob smacked.

Only a moment ago, did I view my dad was my hero and I was sure that nobody could top what he said in my defense, instead, my mother won hands-down. My mother took care of business like the Southern belle she is and Max would have been immensely proud. Right at that very moment, I loved her more than anything else in the entire world.

I frantically made my way over to my parents. The tears were streaming down my cheeks as I ran and collapsed in her arms. That night, she saved me from a certain shame that would probably have followed me for years to come.

"I love you, mommy."

I held her snugly against me as the tears continued to gush from my eyes.

"I am so sorry, my lovey."

She backed up slightly and dabbed at the tears on my cheeks, "Don't ever apologize for who you are, my girl. I love you just as you are, okay?"

My father placed his arms around us and held us both firmly against him.

"I love my girls. Damn, the South has seen better days."

We burst out laughing. How I wished Max was there. How I wished even more that Michael was there. I turned around to find Ryan standing where I had left him. I waved and smiled. He seemed lost, bewildered and wholly out of place. When he waved back, he quickly turned away. I was sure going to miss that eight-second cowboy.

"Come on girls, let's go home."

My father's arms were still around us when we huddled arm in arm, back to the truck.

"Really mom? The Wilsons' and the Sandersons'?"

"You betcha! It's been going on for years and I am pretty sure those kids don't know who their fathers are."

I burst out laughing again, and when we reached my father's truck, I just knew from the innermost core of me that we were going to be okay.

Alice VL

I DO (NOT) – AT THE RODEO

The following morning, I was unexpectedly awakened by the ringing of my mobile phone. I struggled to open my eyes and felt groggy, almost as though I had just fallen asleep.

My mobile phone was wailing horrendously next to me, and when I grabbed it from my pedestal, I answered irritably without first looking at the caller ID. I felt sluggish and exhausted.

"Hey …"

"Ally?"

It was Daniel's voice at the other end of the call. My heart instantly missed a beat and began to flutter insanely. His voice woke me up at once, and I was secretly thrilled.

"Daniel? Hi."

"Sorry to worry you so early. We've just come from the museum. There was a small fire in the early hours of this morning, but we've managed to put out. I've just left the police station where a Detective Mark Warren suspects arson, and is waiting for my final report."

I was suddenly wide awake and sat straight up in bed,

"A fire? Arson? At the museum?"

"There's no damage to the structure or to any of the artifacts or paintings. Gill has already hired painters, so everything is under control. Detective Warren just needs to see you as soon as possible."

"Wow. Okay. I'll leave in a few hours."

Alice VL

"I can come and get you?"

"No, that's okay. I'll drive back and let you know when I'm there. Do you have any idea who would do such a thing?"

"We figure it's the same gang that set the last fire."

"Alright. I hope they get the guys."

"See you later then. Drive safe."

"Thanks for letting me know. See you later."

I ended the call at once and rolled out of bed. I couldn't imagine who would set fire to a museum and even though I didn't really want to leave my parents just yet, secretly, I missed Daniel and I wanted to see him again.

I slipped on a pair of jeans and a sweater before I started packing my suitcase. When my mom walked in, I could in no way at all, deny the disappointment on her face.

"Are you leaving?"

"Oh mom, I am so sorry. There was a fire at the museum last night and the police need to speak to me. I wish I could send Gill in my place, but she wouldn't know how to handle them. The problem they're having is; it is the second fire in our area and they are pretty sure it is gang-related."

"Well, that's depressing. Never mind, I understand my lovey. Just come visit us soon, okay?"

"I promise, mommy. I won't stay away too long this time. There is nothing better than being home with you and dad."

Alice VL

I DO (NOT) – AT THE RODEO

She lovingly embraced me before my dad walked in, "You're leaving?"

"I know dad. I don't want to, but I must go sort things out at the museum. I've just been telling mom that there was a fire this morning, and a detective Warren or someone wants to interview me. Maybe you and mom can come up to Willow County for a few days?"

"Well. Maybe. It's difficult leaving the farm alone."

"I guess. I'll come back soon, daddy. Thank you and mommy for everything. I love you guys." My dad held me protectively against him. I couldn't help but feel as though the world had come to a standstill. There was nothing in the world that could compare to my father's arms around me at that very moment.

After a quick breakfast, my parents walked me out to my car before I hesitated. I truly wanted to stay. I wanted to spend more time with them and I hated that they would face the folks in Water Hills without me. I wanted to say goodbye to Ryan. I didn't want to leave like that especially after what happened the previous night.

More than anything, I didn't want the townsfolk to assume that I was running away and give them the satisfaction of winning. When I slid into the driver's seat, I turned to look back at my parents, "I haven't told Ryan yet. Will you please tell him I had to go back? And don't let the townsfolk think I ran away daddy please. It's not fair to Ryan."

"Sure baby. Just drive safely and call us when you get

there. Don't you worry about Ryan, he is a tough one and you know your mama won't let them run their mouths from their double-wide's."

My dad squeezed my shoulder and smiled at me. I knew, as I sat there saying goodbye to the two of them; I knew that I was going to miss them dearly.

"I will dad. Love you. And thank you, daddy …"

My eyes trailed over to my mom who was standing next to him, her arm slotted in his. She was sad and when I noticed the tears shimmering in her eyes, my stomach made a wild turn and my heart skipped another beat.

"Bye mommy. I love you. Thank you for everything, mama … I am going to miss you so much."

"Love you too, my lovey. Be safe."

I forced a weak smile and waved before I pulled away. As I drove through the tree-lined driveway of the farm, I glanced back through the rearview mirror. They were still standing in the distance, waving. I watched as my mother swabbed at the tears on her cheeks. When my father placed his arm around her, I smiled and knew instantly that they would be just fine. We were all going to be just fine.

Alice VL

It was a long, tedious drive back to Willow County. I reflected on the past week and I thought about Max. I thought back to how Max's passing changed us all from the moment he left us.

I thought back to the days that my mother refused to climb out of bed, and how my father would beg her to come back to him. I thought about Heather and the folks of Water Hills. I smiled often when I thought about my mother and how she put a sock up each of their butts.

I was still gob smacked by their secrets, and suddenly didn't feel as ashamed as I did the night before. When I drove into Willow County, I was happy to be home and excited to see Daniel again. As much as I was going to miss my parents, I was happy to be back and be able to pick up where I left off. I pulled up to a stop sign, and quickly dialed Daniel from my mobile,

"I'm here … where to now?"

"I'll meet you at the precinct."

"Okay."

When I pulled away, I turned right in the direction the police station, which was barely two miles from where I was. I turned into a parking right in front of the station, and switched off my car, sure that Daniel couldn't possibly be there yet.

I waited. I didn't want to go in without him. Barely a few minutes later, he pulled up in his truck, and parked right in front of me. My soul smiled, and I was instantly aware of my racing heart. That lasted only a second; it lasted only until I saw her climb out of his passenger seat. My heart dropped right there and then.

'Ouch.'

While opening my door, I hesitated at first, but climbed out anyways. The disappointment I was feeling into the very core of me was tremendous and categorically unexpected. My insides hurt and a lump in my throat began to unkindly hamper my ability to speak, breathe or swallow with ease.

A forced smile was the best I could offer when they walked up to me. I was entirely caught off-guard by the woman standing in front of me, and who was smiling from ear to year while clutching possessively onto Daniel's arm.

'Can't she stand up on her own?'

She was young, much younger than I was. I thought her to be in her early twenties, but certainly not a day over twenty-five.

Her long, flowing and perfectly styled blonde hair was flawless, but when I looked into her icy blue eyes, I understood at once how she could quite easily have bowled Daniel over. She was beautiful; just like a porcelain doll. She was perfect.

Her skin reminded me of chinaware and her smile radiated nothing but beauty and warmth. I unwittingly scrutinized her from top to bottom and was convinced that her waist, hips and chest were the perfect permutation. I suddenly couldn't hide the sense of feeling boring, drab and ugly standing in front of her.

I DO (NOT) – AT THE RODEO

Daniel must have seen the utter desolation on my face, and immediately placed his arms around me, and warmly hugged me. While holding me for just a moment longer than would be deemed as acceptable, I couldn't help but become aware of an honesty to his touch. 'I know. I've been told that I wear my heart on my sleeve. I can't help it.'

"Welcome back."

"Thanks."

I could barely look him in the eye. I was mad at him. At once, I berated myself again for the unknown emotions that were beginning to annihilate me and leave me senseless.

"This is Lucy."

'Woozy.' When she extended a perfectly manicured hand out to me and smiled, I at once detected a glistening in her eyes. I didn't want to take her hand. I didn't want to feel what Daniel feels, but I did, and I reluctantly shook her hand. 'Just as I thought, way too soft and petite for Daniel.'

"I'm Ally."

"I know. Daniel's told me so much about you."

'He has?' I frowned and glared back at Daniel. 'What did he tell her?'

"Good things, I hope?"

She giggled awkwardly before she placed a way-too-soft hand on his shoulder, "He says you're the sister he never had."

I DO (NOT) – AT THE RODEO

'What the hell? The sister he never had?' I glanced over to him and instinctively, scowled at him. Anger and frustration was beginning to build up inside of me, and I didn't quite know how to put a lid on it. 'His sister? 'Daniel bowed his head, unable to look me in the eye. He was uncomfortable, fidgety and far too quiet.

"Amway, should we go in?"

"Yep, this way."

The relief on Daniel's face was unmistakable when he turned to make his way into the precinct. Lucy was still clutching his hand and walked close to him while I kept my distance, and followed them inside.

I hated that he brought Lucy woozy. According to what my mind was telling me, she was a bimbo and probably has the IQ of my shoe size. I didn't like her. One. Little. Bit. More than anything, I didn't like the fact that Daniel thought her significant enough to bring her along. To meet me.

We had barely walked through the door when a tall, dark and rough-looking man wearing and old pair of scuffed jeans, a T-shirt and a holster approached us.

"Hi Daniel. Did you manage to get a hold of Miss Bradshaw?"

"Yep …"

He turned around at once and took me by my arm, "She just got back from Constantia."

Alice VL

I DO (NOT) – AT THE RODEO

I slowly gazed up at the rough-looking man standing in front of me; an entire head taller than Daniel. He smiled, and offered me an extended hand,

"Hi. I'm Mark Warren. Detective. Sorry to have cut your vacation short."

'Oh, my hat.' That voice. Deep. Croaky. Husky. It matched his appearance and form perfectly, which I might add, was nothing short of perfect. Even his scruffy three-day-old beard was largely appealing and I was pleasantly surprised.

I took his hand and shook it as firmly as I could. I wanted him to know that I was tough'ish too. Sort of. But, definitely not like little Lucy over there that could snap like a twig if she was handled just a tad bit too brusquely.

His hands were as coarse and tough as his appearance, and I was secretly hoping that he was a little on the selfish side too.

'Above the law, I hope.'

Still, I was no butch. I was still a lady; classy and elegant who just says fuck a lot, so I smiled reservedly. 'Oh Lord. There goes my leg again.' I was beginning to sway slightly again, side to side, back and forth while cradling my handbag in front of me.

"That's no problem. Work comes first."

'Lucy. Lucy who? She can have Daniel, for now.' Glancing over at Daniel, I knew that I was doing nothing more than trying to fool myself. A slight tang bust through my heart when I unintentionally pictured Daniel and Lucy together. Like that. 'Not now, Ally.' Instead of lingering in the unwelcomed emotions Daniel was responsible for, I rubbished him, and I rubbished Lucy. I was determined to focus on this rough boy who left me grinning from ear to ear. 'Detective Mark Warren … I can't wait to get detectiving with you.' Oh. Lord. Detectiving? Really?

Alice VL

ALMOST THE END!

I must say, this must have been by far the most exhaustive and emotionally trying period in my life since my divorce from Michael. Nevertheless, it was something I had to deal with and get out of the way, and I am glad I did. Mission accomplished!

I think the breakthrough I had with my parents was long overdue, and even though we'll never quite recover from losing Max, I know deep into my soul that we can move forward from his death and start picking up and mending those broken and fragmented shards again.

I still have my dream with Max on my mind, as though he was actually there. I spend much time shedding a tear or two when I think back to that night. It still hurts. It will always hurt. I will search for Max on empty beaches and crowded streets every single day of the week. But, I know that Max is everywhere and all around us. I have to have faith in that. I have to trust him. I am constantly reminded of his opinion of my fireman. We'll see what the future has in store for us; if there even will be an 'us.'

How about my mama, huh? I am not going to lie, I did not see that one coming, but when she started pulling those stuck-up, snobbish bitches and bulls apart, I couldn't have asked for better entertainment. Wow! You all should have seen my dad's face! Aah. You had to be there.

Speaking of which, I hated that he walked in on Ryan and I, but, I saw a side to my father that I never thought I'd ever see! It was awesome! It was the one thing that made me see my daddy as my hero again. Although, still deathly awkward.

Drool and then there's Ryan. Let me tell you, Ryan was a once-in-a-lifetime encounter. He was a fifteen out of ten. I think my body fell in love with him after our very first 'meeting;' just a pity my heart doesn't dance to the same tune.

Ryan has amazing sex appeal, and it didn't take much to be wildly drawn in by him as I was so easily transported from peak to peak. Perhaps, my animal instincts and his honey-suckling scent was enough to bypass all foreplay. We were hanky-pankying every chance we got. There's that damn word again. I can't get it out of my system. Thanks Heather!

With Heather on my mind, I know it was she who set us up, but I am going to let it slide. I haven't told my dad simply because I don't really want the long arm of the law to come down on her. Not only is she pregnant, but Max once loved her. She has gone through much after Max died, and I am happy, okay, a little happy that she is moving on with her life. I wish her all the best. I do. Sort of.

Daniel. I don't know anymore where to place Daniel. I don't know exactly how he fits into my life, but wherever it is, I am just not ready for any of it. I don't like Lucy woozy. I don't think she is a good fit for Daniel, but I am not holding my breath. I am pretty sure he will tire of her soon. I hope. Stop Ally.

Alice VL

I realize that I am a little too fond of Daniel, I know that and I know I am bringing more trouble on myself because of it. But, what I still like is discovering how sex with different men are exactly that, different. Speaking of sex, I can't wait to see what happens with Detective Mark Warren.

I hope my body approves, and I truly hope, more than anything, that he doesn't disappoint. Look at him, he is hot. But, more of that in the next installment, Above The Law.

See you next time guys!

Just don't call me drab, boring or ugly.

Ally!

Alice VL